There Is No Death in *Finding Nemo*

Stories

By

Jeffrey M. Feingold

D1437967

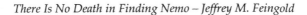

For my daughter, Hannah Feingold, the rich girl who brought me what money can't buy.

OTHER TITLES BY IMPSPIRED

Shrinking to Fit –
by John Eagles

Menopausal Mermaids & Life Lines -
by Sinead Coxhill

Honestly? It Never Bothered Me –
by John Doyle

Each Imaginary Arrow -
by Scott Ferry

Rueful –
by Kathleen Denizard

The Bones of the Story –
by Sandra Arnold

Magic Cube of Time –
by Vatsala Radhakeesoon

Acknowledgements

There Is No Death in *Finding Nemo*, published by Maudlin House. Copyright 2023 by Jeffrey M. Feingold.

The Mirror, published by Meat for Tea. Copyright 2023 Jeffrey M. Feingold

The Box, published by Choeofpleirn Press. Copyright 2023 by Jeffrey M. Feingold

Rich Girl, published by Superlative literary journal. Copyright 2022 by Jeffrey M. Feingold.

The Loneliest Number, published by After Dinner Conversations. Copyright 2022 by Jeffrey M. Feingold.

CONTENTS

THE NARCISSIST'S LIBRARY

A tree-lined parkway serpentined for miles along the center of the City, dividing affluent neighborhoods north from the indigent south. During the long northern winters, the thick barren tree limbs were brown. In spring they suddenly sprouted, exploding into a leafy dark green canopy, which, on windy days, hissed softly as a snake.

The parkway was a narrow vein of modest but well-kept middle-class bungalows, townhouses, duplexes, and three-and four-story brick apartment buildings, separating two close yet disparate worlds. North of the parkway lived doctors, dentists, lawyers, and politicians, with Botox smiles, and designer dogs. Their BMWs and Bentleys were garaged behind wrought iron gates of tony mansions, walled off by the parkway from the ramshackle south, with its trailers and tenement apartments. Here lived transients and immigrants— cooks, bussers, retail clerks, and gig workers, their rusting beaters and bicycles dotting the rutted roads, where mongrel dogs fought for trash can scraps.

Occasionally these two worlds momentarily meshed, when the well-heeled opened the wrought iron gates of their northern enclaves, to venture forth, dressed in their finery, to the trendy parkway cafes and bistros serviced by the poor.

It was in just one such vegetarian bistro that

11

Dakota first met Zayden in spring. She was waiting tables, to help put herself through the music conservatory, just next door, where she studied violin under the esteemed maestro, the great Jascha Milstrakh. Dakota was five foot four, with shoulder length chestnut hair, a comely face, and large nut-brown eyes. She was a woman who appeared quiet and soft on the outside, yet she had a strong core of independence and resolve. She wore a new fitted black tee-shirt with a silk-screened violin, with the words beneath, 24 *Caprices for Solo Violin, Niccolò Paganini*.

Zayden, a handsome, dark figure, was sitting alone in the bistro, pretending to read a hardcover edition of *Lives of the Great Composers*. He ordered a salad and iced tea for lunch. Just as Dakota began to turn away from his table, he said, "Paganini was misunderstood." The two struck up a conversation.

After lunch, Zayden—a commercial real estate developer—walked back to the conservatory bookstore.

"I want to return this for a refund," he said, handing *Lives of the Great Composers* to the cashier.

"You just bought it a little over an hour ago," the cashier said, having been the same employee who had sold the book to Zayden that morning.

"Yes, I'm aware of that," Zayden said, "I know when I bought the book. Do I look stupid, to you?"

"I'm sorry, it's just—"

"It's just not that great," Zayden said, "that's what it's just not. I mean, they weren't so *great* really, were they, the 'Great Composers'? All they wrote was boring shit. Not exactly The Beatles or Imagine Dragons. Besides, the book served its purpose."

"Huh?" said the clerk.

"I got a date."

"I don't follow," said the clerk.

"What else are books for? Oh, can I ask you something—that is, if it's not too *stupid* for you?"

"OK, I guess."

"Where can I get a steak around here? I'm starving. All they have next door is rabbit food."

After this day, there were many meals that spring and summer at the same bistro. And many books purchased from, then summarily returned to, the conservatory bookstore. Yet despite his fundamental baseness, Zayden was quite capable of engaging in banter—even witty repartee—with Dakota. He also eventually began to keep some of the music books he bought, and to read them, although he disliked reading.

Zayden was brimming with confidence and enthusiasm, which Dakota, a shy, somewhat anxious young woman, found compelling, even mysterious. Each was born and raised in the parkway, although Zayden was ten years Dakota's elder.

Whereas Zayden had dated extensively, Dakota had dated only musicians until now. They were always so terribly needy—musicians—such moody, incompetent little boys. They struggled with the simplest things. How to show up on time. How to dress appropriately. How to act responsibly. But to Dakota, Zayden seemed to be a man. After a brief courtship, Zayden suggested to Dakota that they move in together in the fall. Dakota's older sister, Mary, warned against the move.

"I mean, Jesus, Cody," Mary said on the phone one afternoon, when Zayden was in Buffalo on a work trip, "you hardly know this guy. Here a date, there a date, then you're moving in together. What if, you know, he's one of those axe murderers or stranglers or something, like on *Crime Watch*? You do watch *Crime Watch*, don't you, Cody?"

"I don't think so," Dakota said. "He's a sweet guy, Sis. Besides, you and Phil only dated for about six months before you got married."

"Cody, honey," Mary said, "Phil and I, well, we aren't doing so hot."

"Everyone I know sees a couple's counselor at some point," Dakota said.

"I think we're getting a divorce," Mary said.

***

Zayden had ambition. His sights were set on

those fine northern mansions. That's where *I* should be, he often said to Dakota, as they strolled hand-in hand along the parkway. Purgatory Parkway, Zayden called it. Theirs was a whirlwind romance. Despite Mary's protests, they moved in together, in the fall, while Dakota was still at the conservatory. They took up residence on the ground floor of a tidy brick parkway apartment building. Just Zayden, Dakota, and her cat, named after the composer, Arnold Schoenberg.

Zayden was not fond of cats.

"Jesus, he sounds like he's dying," Zayden said whenever the cat meowed.

"I know," Dakota said, "it's just that he's atonal."

Zayden tolerated the cat, perhaps because he traveled much for work. His book of business grew. He was the kind of businessman businessmen liked. Handsome, self-assured, garrulous.

Since their finances were so good, Dakota hired a house cleaner that fall. She wanted to focus on her studies, and practice for her upcoming recital. She also joined a book club, since Zayden was often away, and she was a little lonely when he traveled. The club members took turns hosting readings at their residences each week.

***

Fall turned into winter, and again the thick branches of the parkway trees turned brown. Then, the next spring, not long after new leaves sprouted along the parkway trees, just when Dakota felt the impending explosion of green, life took a strange turn. An invisible, unwelcomed visitor—a microbe—entered the City. It coursed through the vein of the parkway, spreading out quickly across all the neighborhoods north and south. People grew afraid. From where had this pestilence come? Was it unnatural? Had it escaped from a government laboratory? Had immigrants brought it?

Soon the cafes and bistros were shuttered, by order of the City Manager. The wrought iron gates of the northern mansions remained locked. People everywhere avoided each other. Zayden had to travel further and further from home to locales the contagion had not yet reached.

Zayden's business suffered. Dakota trimmed their budget where she could. She stopped buying sheet music. Classes were now online because of the pestilence, so she sold her Subaru. She let the housekeeper go, too, and cleaned house herself. She thought Zayden could also help clean, when he was home from his work travels, but he always said, "I'm exhausted from the road, Cody. I can't move a muscle." Then he'd sprawl on the sofa to watch sports on television while she cleaned.

"Just don't clean in my office," Zayden said, when Dakota first let go the housekeeper. "I've got Very Important Papers for work all over."

Dakota was cleaning one morning, while Zayden

16

was with a client in Poughkeepsie, which was not yet under a cloud of contagion. Here, Arnie Arnie Arnie, she called. She always put the cat in the bathroom and closed the door before vacuuming the living room, since atonal Arnold was terrified of the more atonal, screeching Hoover. Dakota looked under the bed. No Arnold. She looked in the bathroom. In the kitchen. Under the sofa. Arnold apparently had vanished. Here, Arnie Arnie Arnie, she called again. Then she saw the door to Zayden's office was open more than a crack. She walked over and opened the door further. There was Arnold, standing on Zayden's desk, next to his antique typewriter. A cat as black as night, standing in bright sunshine streaming in from the skylight.

Arnold stood between two tall white stacks of Zayden's Very Important Papers. What a great photo this would make, Dakota mused. Arnie the Sun God! How she adored him. Arnold stared at Dakota with all the sweetness there is in the universe. Then, nonchalantly— as if he'd very nearly forgotten, but at last remembered there was something he had to do—lifted his tail to pee on the side of one of the stacks of the Very Important Papers. Oh, no, Arnie! You come here this minute! Arnold stared at Dakota. He appeared to understand her. Then he adjusted his position slightly, lifted his tail, and began to spray the other stack. Arnold was nothing if not thorough.

After securing Arnold in the bathroom, Dakota got the roll of paper towels from the kitchen counter and hurried back to Zayden's office. She dabbed the pee papers as much as possible. She thought she could place the damp papers on the floor of the office, all around the braided rug, to let them dry fully. But when she looked down at the rug, she saw that it was filthy. She vacuumed it, then began to roll it up to bring it outside to shake out. As she rolled up the rug, Dakota made a startling discovery. She saw in the floor a handle, with hinges across from it. A trap door. She wondered if some prior tenant hid valuables in the floor. She slid her index finger underneath the little silver clasp, then pulled the heavy door open.

To her surprise, she saw not a horde of gold, but rather several rows of small photo albums, their spines facing up, each spine labeled in printed black letters. Sitting cross-legged on the floor by the secret library, she picked up the first book in the first row. It was labeled "Abby" on the spine.

On the first page of the book of Abby, taped to the lined paper, was a photograph of an attractive, buxom young woman. Beneath the photo appeared the words— in text which looked to be from a typewriter—"Back seat of her father's Buick Riviera. Twice. Comfortable seats— velour. Loves kissing—no tongues. Talks too much. Gabby Abby." Below these lines of text were more lines: "Loves sports, especially football. Three times in the woods behind the stadium. *Very* passionate. Touchdown! Four and one-quarter stars." The detailed notes went on for some length.

From Dakota's frozen hands the book slipped

18

back into the hole from where it had come. Dakota uttered not a word nor moved a muscle. It was as if she were in a trance. It is possible these books belong to a prior tenant. Zayden must not know these are here. Why would he? The notes appear to have been typewritten. Can Zayden even use a typewriter? I've never seen him type on one. Who still knows how to use a typewriter of all things? Yes, these must be from someone who lived here before.

But she knew. Somehow—she knew. Something about Zayden's self-confidence. The way he walked. How he often stood on the balls of his feet, hands on his hips, grinning. His perfectly pomaded pompadour, the black hair in front swept up like a salute, flanked by slick short sides. It was all too perfect. Too controlled. Too tight. A highly varnished veneer concealing the rot within. Yes, she knew. She supposed that she had always known.

Finally, Dakota stirred, and looked into the secret library. She picked up Abby's neighbor, the book of Alicia. She opened the photo album cover. Alicia was tall, thin, golden-haired, and bronzed-limbed. "Loves art" was the note beneath her photo. "Stuffy, uptight. Once in art gallery. Two stars." As in Abby's book, the notes about Alicia went on in further detail. After Alicia came Brenda, who received but one star.

After Brenda came Brianna, then Brielle, then Brooke. My God, they're in alphabetical order. He's *alphabetized* them! Each woman, her photos, the lurid details, the ratings. *Ratings*. After Brooke came Cassie

19

("five times, four and a half stars, a total volcano"). After Cassie was Christine. Then, after Christine—Dakota's world froze. She felt the Earth stop turning on its axis. She opened the next cover, gazed upon a photo of herself in her Paganini tee, and read the words beneath: "Classical musician. Nerdy type. Submissive. Several times in the parkway. Five, maybe six times in her Subaru. Seats too small, but worth the ride. Five stars, even though I had to read that stupid book about the great composers."

Dakota had only opened the books up to her name. To the right of where she picked up her book were books for women with names beginning with letters further up the alphabet. Dozens more notebooks in the secret library. Next to the names of some of the women were the numbers of their apartments in Dakota's apartment building. All the way up to Stacy, Apartment 3B ("two stars"); Wanda, Apartment 4A ("a nurse, one and one-half stars"); and Valerie, Apartment 4C ("flight attendant, twice in the airport lounge after hours, four and a half stars, a firecracker"). Dakota placed all the books back, closed the secret door, and rolled the rug back in place. She cried. Then screamed. Then swore. Then cried.

***

"I knew it. I just *knew*. I said he was no good," Mary said on the phone. "That's what I said, isn't it? Oh, poor baby, have you been crying? *Bastard*. No, Phil, not *you*, for God's sake. I wasn't talking about you. What? No,

20

we can't do it tonight, for Christ's sake, I'm on the *phone* with my sister. No, Phil, that's not why. Why? Because we're getting a *divorce*, Phil, that's why. It's not what divorced couples do, is it? Christ, put a sock on it! I mean—"

"Mary?" Dakota said.

"Oh, I'm so sorry, honey."

"That's OK," Dakota said. She sat on the edge of her bed, patting Arnold. With her other hand, she pressed the speaker button on her smartphone, and placed it on the bed.

"You need to cut it off," Mary said.

"The relationship?"

"No, his penis. No, Phil, not yours, *his*. Just go away, will you? Get in your Jeep and drive. I'm sorry honey, do you feel any better?"

Pulling a sock on one foot, as he hopped on the other, Phil hollered from the bedroom, well, yes, I will go for a ride in my Jeep, why not, but Dakota should just dump Zayden. Tell her to just dump him, Mary, that's what she should do. Alright, Mary, yes, I'm going. Yes, I know it's not what divorced people do. I mean, we're not divorced, yet. I'll be back later. We should talk about this, Mary. No, not about Dakota, about you and me. OK, goodbye. Just dump him, Dakota, don't take it lying down. Don't let him walk all over you!

After the call, Dakota decided to go for a walk for some fresh air. She stood up from the edge of the bed. She took her door keys and wallet from her nightstand. She paused, then picked up Arnold with two hands and hugged him to her chest. Arnie, my sweet boy! She carried him out of the bedroom, across the living room, and into Zayden's office. She carefully placed Arnold on top of Zayden's desk, next to stacks of Very Important Papers. She gently lifted Arnold's tail.

Dakota walked out of the office, then across the living room, to the front door. I thought we'd get married someday. Have children. Grandchildren. A life. It's all just a lie. The relationship. The future together. The love. One big, stinking, sucking wind lie. She didn't have enough composure to compose herself. She walked out of her apartment in her blue satin pajamas and her fluffy slippers, her hair a fright. Who cares, anyway?

In the hallway, she tried to lock her apartment door, but fumbled with the key. Although she had locked the door a thousand times, she could not remove the key from the lock. She began to cry. She slid to the floor, sobbing. After a few minutes, her neighbor across the hall, in apartment 1B, peeked his head out of his doorway.

"Ms. Dakota, you are alright? You are maybe crying?" said Mr. Bernstein.

Dakota continued to sob. Mr. Bernstein walked to her.

"Let me help you up," said Mr. Bernstein. "Why don't you have some tea, Ms. Dakota. My tea you always like. I will fix a nice cup. Come, come," he said, helping her rise slowly up.

"If you wish, Ms. Dakota, I can wear a mask," Mr. Bernstein said, "because, on the one hand, this is what news says to do."

He walked arm in arm with Dakota into his flat.

"On the other hand, I haven't seen no one since this bug, so with me you are safe. Of course, on one hand, who knows, what is safe? On the other hand, with me, you are safe."

He made two cups of black tea while Dakota sat at his small round kitchen table, running an index finger back and forth on the smooth white linoleum top. She was no longer sobbing.

Mr. Bernstein didn't like too much silence.

"It's a funny thing," he said, "Edna, God rest, she loves this dinette, always. It was part of a set for a play, in the Yiddish Theater. That's how we met. She was beautiful on stage. Such an actress. Such an angel. So here it is. I keep it, this set, even though it's from maybe 1950."

Dakota did not speak.

"Sometimes, we have tea. I know, I know, yes, she's dead, God rest. But here I sit, in this chair, and we have our talks. She loves this set."

Still, Dakota did not speak.

"And then what, Ms. Dakota? You, I will tell what. I feel better, that's what's what. So, you see, Ms. Dakota, to talk is good. That is why I talk, to Edna."

Dakota looked at Mr. Bernstein. She ran the tip of her right index finger along the warm porcelain rim of the teacup as she looked at his moist, kind, ocean-blue eyes.

"Maybe to me you also talk," he said.

"Alright, Mr. Bernstein," Dakota said.

"Please, Ms. Dakota," he said, "always you call me, Mr. Bernstein. Tonight, maybe you call me, Aleksey."

"Alright, Mr. Bernstein," Dakota said.

"Good!" Mr. Bernstein said, "now we are talking."

And Dakota did talk. She talked, and she felt better. She told Mr. Bernstein–Aleksey–the whole sordid story. They had cup after cup of tea. Mr. Bernstein was glad to listen, for he had been suspicious of Zayden for some time. Zayden would holler loudly in the hallway, outside of Mr. Bernstein's apartment. Shut that stupid pug up! I'm sick and tired of your little shit dog! One afternoon, Mr. Bernstein had been taking Kugel the Pug for a walk. Kugel was behind Mr. Bernstein as he locked his apartment door. When he heard Kugel shriek horribly, he turned just in time to see Zayden lowering his boot onto the floor after, Mr. Bernstein was sure, kicking Kugel. He couldn't prove it. But he knew in his heart what kind of man Zayden was.

As they talked and drank and cried and laughed, an idea was taking hold within Dakota. Look at this man. This beautiful man. He and Edna had been married for fifty years, until Edna died. And still, he talks to her. I deserve love like that. I will find it. I will find that love. I will go out, into this world, and find where it is waiting for me. But first …

***

As did most of the apartments in Dakota's building, the door to Apartment 3B had a little wooden table next to it. On this table was a small white figurine of a ragdoll cat. Next to the cat was a stack of business cards from The Humane Society of The United States. Behind the card stack was a framed photo of a woman sitting in a room with dozens of cats. The photo was labelled, Parkway Cat Shelter.

Dakota knocked on the door, just below the name card, printed in neat, black, capital letters. **STACY ALNAUGHT**. The knock was answered by meowing. A great deal of meowing. Dakota knocked again. The only reply was meowing. The package Dakota then placed on the table was wrapped in plain brown paper. It was the size of a small photo album. Dakota slipped a note, sealed in an envelope, under the door.

There was no meowing when Dakota knocked on the door to apartment 4A. There was a little wooden table, but it was empty. There was no name on the card on the door. Only the letter W. A small round sticker next to the W said, Nurses Save Lives. Dakota knocked again. Silence. She felt a little sad. She slipped the wrapped photo book onto the table, pushed the sealed envelope under the door, and walked on.

At this point, Dakota wanted to go home. She'd just slip the photo album on the table by Apartment 4C, slide the letter under the door, and leave, without knocking. But when she arrived at 4C, there was no place to put the book. The table was full. Small snow globes covered every inch of the table. The snow globes were all labeled with exotic locales from across the globe. Bangkok. London. Paris. Venice. Wichita. Then the door opened and out stepped a tall, lean woman, in a navy-blue uniform with a blood red pinstripe, black stockings, red shoes to match the pinstripe, and a white face mask with an airplane logo. She wore a matching blue hat with a metal pin in the shape of wings. The two women looked at each other.

"I'm Dakota, from 1A downstairs."

Valerie the flight attendant's face went white as her face mask, so white it seemed that all her blood had drained down into her red shoes.

"I don't want to keep you," Dakota said, "but I wanted to give you this."

She handed the wrapped photo album and the sealed envelope to Valerie.

26

"I, I don't have a lot of time," Valerie said, taking the book and envelope. "I have to catch a flight in a bit. I'm a flight attendant with Jet Bird."

"Yes, I know," Dakota said, "I read your book."

Although Valerie didn't know why, there was something about Dakota, about her face, the expression, the openness, which made her invite Dakota in. The two women sat at Valerie's kitchen dinette table. Dakota told Valerie the whole, sordid story. At the end, Dakota said, looking at the book on the table, "this one is yours, it's about you. From his secret library."

"Oh, I see," Valerie said.

Dakota pushed back the vinyl dinette chair. The metal legs squeaked on the linoleum kitchen floor.

"I hope you'll come," Dakota said, looking down at Valerie, still seated at the dinette table. "On Saturday. Ten o'clock."

***

"I don't get it, babe," Zayden said around breakfast time. He was in his pajamas, sprawled on the sofa of the apartment, watching television. He ate slices of cold pepperoni pizza, while Dakota placed napkins and small plates of snacks around the living room.

"You've invited the book club here, this morning? What about the germ? I mean, I don't care, it's mostly fake news anyway. But what about the people in the club?"

"They'll all wear masks," Dakota said.

"I don't know about those snacks, though," Zayden said. "Hummus and veggies? Olives? Fruit? I'd put out something fun, like maybe those little hot dogs, you know, the tiny ones wrapped in pastry. But it's your show, babe."

Zayden stood up from the sofa and walked into his office, leaving the door open.

"I'll be in here 'till your meeting is over," he called out to Dakota.

At ten o'clock the doorbell rang. Several women wearing face masks stood in the hallway. Each held a book in one hand, and a plate of food in the other. Dakota ushered them in. After a few minutes or so of snacking and chitchatting, Dakota said, "well, why don't we begin."

"I'll start," a woman said after removing her face mask.

She was sitting on the sofa. She wore a black tee shirt with a picture of an open book, and the words, If My Book Is Open, Your Mouth Should Be Shut. She placed her plate of snacks on the coffee table. She picked up her book from the table, stood, and began reading.

"The Book of Valerie," she read, quite loudly— nearly at the top of her voice. "She is a flight attendant, for Jet Bird airlines."

Valerie paused for a moment in response to the loud clattering sound from Zayden's office. Then she continued, even more loudly than before, "twice in the airport lounge, after hours. Four and a half stars."

Again, the sound of clattering was heard, as Zayden tripped over the office trash can. Valerie remained undeterred.

"She was a firecracker. A *real* firecracker."

Some more clattering, then Zayden appeared at the threshold of his office. He leaned heavily against the doorframe and stared silently at the group, his mouth open. Valerie sat back down on the sofa.

"I'll go next," another woman said.

She removed her mask, rose from the sofa, book in hand. She was short, full of figure, with closely cropped black hair. Her gray tee shirt had text above and below the picture of a puppy standing by a stack of books. The text above said, "A Woman Cannot Survive On Books Alone." Beneath the picture was the text, "She Also Needs a Dog."

Opening her book to the first page, she read, "The Book of Wanda … a nurse, one and one-half stars."

Zayden stumbled backwards into his office, tripping on the trashcan and falling onto the floor.

As the readings continued, Zayden resumed his position at the office threshold, leaning now against the doorframe to prevent himself from slumping back down to the floor. He could not have looked paler had he been a snack at Dracula's holiday party.

There was a knock at the front door. Dakota walked over and let in Mr. Bernstein. He slowly ambulated over to Zayden.

"I'll tell you what, young man" Mr. Bernstein said, looking up, nose to nose with Zayden, who was several inches taller but looking down at Mr. Bernstein. "This thing you have done," he said, his voice rising and cracking, "is a bad thing. That's what. A bad thing. You hurt people. This we do not allow."

Zayden winced as Mr. Bernstein spoke while holding one of the photo books in his right hand. He held the book up to Zayden's face. "Shall I teach you Yiddish, Mr. Smarty Pants? You know what is a schmuck? You are a schmuck. You know what it means, a schmuck? It means a contemptible person is what. A *contemptible* person. That's what's what."

Zayden wanted to recoil back into the office. His mind held only one thought, a singular desire. Flight. But his limbs felt like logs. The women were staring at him. He felt as exposed as an oyster which had been shucked. And still, Mr. Bernstein went on and on, like a sad trombone.

"Also, a meshugana," Mr. Bernstein said. "That

means crazy person. Shame on you, Mr. Meshugana. Mr. Smarty Pants. Mr. Schmuck. Shame! If my Edna, God rest, were here, she'd—"

Zayden could bear this no longer. With both hands, he pushed hard against Mr. Bernstein. He wanted only to move him out of the way, so that he could flee. But so urgent was the push, Mr. Bernstein fell backwards to the floor, hitting his head with a great *whump*. Zayden was horrified. He looked down, saw blood trickling from a corner of the mouth of Mr. Bernstein, whose eyes were closed. The blood ran onto the floor as one of the book club members—Wanda, from Apartment 4A, a nurse ("one and half stars") —bolted upright from the sofa and ran to Mr. Bernstein. She placed two fingers on one side of his neck.

After a few moments, Wanda looked up at Zayden's terrified, colorless face. She shook her head slowly from side to side. Zayden knew what this meant. Mr. Bernstein was gone. He dashed to the front door, into the hallway, and out of the apartment building. He began running along the parkway toward the subway station a few blocks down. Although the air was cool, he sweated profusely. How could this happen? To me? I had everything, everything under control. As he ran along, he thought about prison. I can't do it. I can't go. I'm too— good looking. Too boyish. I won't make it.

Back at the apartment, Mr. Bernstein began to smile, then softly chuckle. He spat out what remained of the kryolan capsule in his mouth. He'd bitten on the

31

capsule hard when Zayden pushed him. Mr. Bernstein's saliva then mixed with the powdered fake stage blood in the capsule and the liquid had run out of his mouth.

"Let me help you up," Wanda said, as Mr. Bernstein began to rise from the floor.

"Oh, I'm fine, thank you, fine. What a show! I wish my Edna was here to see. This she should see. She was so beautiful, you know, on the stage. The Yiddish Theater. Do you know it? Edna, she was a beauty. Me, not so much."

"Oh, Mr. Bernstein," Dakota said, "you're the most beautiful man I know."

***

Nearing the subway station, Zayden knew he had to escape far from the City. He could never return. He would flee to a faraway place, change his name, never look back. There would be new bistros, new bookstores, new women in a new place.

It was springtime. Running along at full tilt, his heart near to bursting, Zayden looked up. The tree limbs had exploded into a leafy dark green canopy, which, on this windy day, hissed softly as a snake.

THE MIRROR

At six o'clock, after helping Lara clean up the supper dishes, Mark, alone in the den, took off all his clothes. He had been sitting on the armchair in the den of their farmhouse, reading the local weekly paper, the *Egremont Insider*, when, in an instant, the newsprint went fuzzy. He removed his bifocals, held them up to the light slanting in from the open window facing Lara's iris garden. The bearded iris, which normally only bloom in spring and summer, were blooming for a second time, off-season, in late September. It had been an exceptionally hot, dry summer–the hottest ever recorded–and Lara worried if the stress had damaged the plants.

"The planet is dying," she said, "my flowers are confused."

"Try not to worry," Mark had said to her, in his congenial bedside manner, "sometimes, there's no clear explanation."

Mark's glasses, neither scratched nor smudged, were the same pair he had read the *Insider* with every Sunday evening for five years, since he and Lara bought the farmhouse. Mark placed the glasses back on. The words on the newspaper appeared wavy and indistinct, as if someone had left the paper out in the rain. He removed the glasses again, then held up the paper. He could read every word.

Mark was a tall, strong, handsome dermatologist. But with his sixty-fifth birthday just days away, he brooded about aging. Throughout the year, he fought an increasing apprehension. He went to the gym; rode his bike to his office in downtown Egremont; ate light, vegetarian meals; still, whenever he placed his hands on his stomach, there was always more there than before.

"It's like a Stephen King novel," he told his wife, holding his stomach one day.

"Oh?" Lara had said. "I'm not a huge King fan, though I loved Morgan Freeman in *Shawshank Redemption*. What a beautiful man."

"A man wakes up," Mark said, "looks in the mirror, sees he's suddenly thicker than before. That's a bad day. Like a Stephen King horror story–*The Thickening*."

Lara smiled. "Well, it happens," she said, "maybe they'll make a movie of it. Morgan Freeman can play you."

Tonight, alone in the den, suddenly, Mark didn't need his bifocals. He placed his hands on his stomach; he felt somehow different. He rose from the chair, unbuttoned his white dress shirt, removed it, then placed it on one arm of the chair. The crisp September breeze from the open window felt invigorating on his bare skin. He stretched his arms out fully, inhaled, exhaled. He suddenly felt great. He could see everything clearly. Lara's Scrabble pieces on the glass coffee table, for instance. He could read the letters on each small Scrabble

34

square. PHEROMONE was spelled out horizontality. Beneath the first letter E, Lara had spelled ENNUI vertically, and beneath the first O, a descending OBSESSION.

Something was different. Mark undid his belt buckle. He unzipped his fly, stepped out of his trousers, slid them to the floor. He sat in the chair to remove his crew socks, then slipped off his boxers. He stood again, all six feet two inches, without a stitch of clothing. His toes tickled as he wiggled them on the round shag rug beneath the armchair. It felt remarkable. He inhaled again, held it for a moment, then exhaled slowly. This felt remarkable, too. Suddenly, everything felt remarkable, as if nothing in his life had before. The breeze on his skin, the cool air, the scent of flowers, all remarkable.

On the opposite wall of the den was the full-length floor mirror which had been there the day they moved in. Mark walked to the mirror. Gazing into the glass, he was pleased to see how fit he looked. His stomach, flat. His abs, lean. The muscles throughout his body, taut. Had the workouts and bike rides finally paid off? His face, which in recent years had become sallow and pitted, was now rosy and smooth. His eyes, usually red and bleary, were now luminous, the irises as blue as the reblooming iris in Lara's garden.

Mark adored Lara. They first met online twenty years earlier. When they met, Mark fell over the cliff edge, unreservedly. He had eyes only for Lara. If every other woman in town stood naked, in front of his office, as he locked the door and turned to hurry home to his beloved, he wouldn't have seen them. Not even the ones who had come for Botox injections, or glycolic acid peels, or liposuction. Lara was his world. When she smiled, hers was the most beautiful smile in history. When she laughed, it was the first laugh. When she uttered a thought, philosophy was born. It had been this way for twenty years.

Mark heard glass shattering, turned to look behind him.

"What in God's name are you doing?" Lara asked, holding a silver fork in her right hand. Beneath her, a muddle of chopped beets, kale, cherry tomatoes, parsley, and shards of the broken white porcelain plate with a gold leaf rim which she had dropped, combined in a color composition which Kandinsky or Klimt might have painted.

"What are you doing?" Lara repeated.

"I'm not sure," Mark said, "I feel great. Just look at me!" he said, gazing again at his image in the mirror. "I've never looked this good, have I? Isn't it remarkable?"

Lara looked at Mark. At the same sallow, pitted face, the same sagging stomach, the same atrophying muscles, she saw every day.

"Mark, are you feeling alright?"

Mark looked in the mirror. He was so fit, he could

almost see his ribs.

"I feel remarkable."

"Stop saying that, honey. You're scaring me."

Lara was leaving for a month later that night. A trip to Uganda, to work with missionaries at a hospital for the poor. Lara wasn't religious, but she loved to travel, and to do good works, especially since retiring from her career in accounting a few years earlier. So, Lara, the agnostic, would be volunteering at a hospital along with twenty traveling nuns. The idea made her both excited and amused. Staring at her naked husband as he stared at his reflection, she wondered if she should cancel her trip. Mark had always been a quirky, absent-minded professor type, with a brilliant mind, and a childlike wonder. This was probably just another flight of fancy. He was probably fine.

"Why don't you get dressed, honey, while I pack my suitcase? Then you can drive me to the airport a little later."

"No. I will not get dressed. People spend their whole lives dressed, and bored, and unremarkable. Then they die. I want to live, naked, and remarkable. You should try it, Lara. Take off your clothes. It's—remarkable!"

"Yes, love, but you might not feel that way in jail. Please, get dressed."

The next morning, Mark awoke alone in the

farmhouse. He put on his terry bathrobe and slippers, shuffled downstairs to the kitchen, made black coffee, sipped while re-reading the Insider in the den. When he felt the breeze from the window, he rose, undid his bathrobe, let it slip to the floor. He flipped off his slippers, then walked, naked, over to the mirror. He looked even trimmer, more radiant, than yesterday.

As he was feeling so fit, he decided to skip his usual oats with berries breakfast and treat himself to pancakes at Mom's Diner. He hadn't eaten there in years. It was a Monday holiday; his office was closed. Instead of riding his bike to Mom's, he decided to take the pickup. No need to overdo the healthy lifestyle now. If anything, the man in the mirror could stand to pack on a pound or two. He walked to the den door leading out to the iris garden, stepped outside, strode to his truck. At the driver's door, he patted the outside of his pants pocket where he kept his keys. He felt his skin, then remembered, there was no pocket where he patted, because he didn't have pants on.

"I don't know, Sis," Lara said into her cellphone. She was sitting at the airport gate, sipping bad coffee, waiting for a connecting flight.

"Well, he's always been a bit quirky," Lara's sister said.

"This feels different," Lara said. "I'm worried. Standing in the den, stark naked, gazing at himself in the mirror."

"Is he taking his medication? Maybe he's depressed

again. If he's not taking his meds, maybe–"

"No, I don't know, Sis. He says it's like being in a Stephen King novel."

"Huh?"

"Getting old. Then he's standing naked in the den, saying he feels remade, or reborn, or remarkable, or some such thing. Maybe I should skip this flight."

"Have you done it lately?"

"Done what?" Lara asked.

"You know, *it*."

"Oh, that," Lara said.

"Well, he's probably OK. You should go on the trip. A break will do you good. He's probably fine. Men act funny. Except for Carl, of course. He's never funny. I don't think dentists are. Funny, that is. Carl's sweet as pie, though, just not funny."

"Yes" Lara said.

"But you should probably do *it* when you get back, Sis. Seriously. Take one for the team, you know?"

"I'll have the double stack," Mark said to the waitress as he sat in the booth at Mom's Diner. "Make that the double stack of blueberry pancakes, lots of maple syrup. Oh, let's try the home fries. With two eggs, over easy. And more coffee–keep it coming!"

After he devoured every bit of food, Mark went to the diner rest room. He looked at the small square mirror above the sink as he scrubbed his hands as some doctors habitually do. Something was wrong. He was peering and squinting at an old man, with yellowish skin, blemishes, a double chin, bloodshot eyes. The mirror was cracked, and flaky, distorting his image. Why would they have such a faulty, shoddy thing on the wall?

He hurried back to his table, paid the bill, and raced back home in the truck. He flung open the unlocked den door and dashed to the mirror. It was clear, now, yes–the diner mirror was corrupted. His den mirror face was flawless. Smooth skin, rosy cheeks, luminous iris eyes. He kept studying his face while he unbuttoned his shirt, removed it, unbuckled his belt, slipped off his trousers and boxers and socks, all the while not diverting his gaze from the handsome mirror man. He stood up straight again to admire the fine, fit figure in the glass.

He stood quite some time, staring at his image. They really should replace that old mirror at Mom's. I'll have to let them know they should do that. Before someone gives themselves a fright. "Yes," he whispered, shaking his head up and down while studying his image, "they really must replace that broken mirror." He stood for a very long while, admiring his reflected perfection.

The doorbell rang.

Mark bounded to the front door, which he flung wide open.

"Well, hello, Finn. Such a gorgeous day!"

Mark's neighbor, Finn O'Brien, a carpenter, stood, silent, and motionless, except for his eyeballs scanning Mark up and down.

"Mark, are you–OK?"

"Never fitter," Mark said. "Why?"

"You're naked."

"Ah, yes," Mark said.

A knowing smirk swam across Finn's broad, scabrous face. "Weed, is it?" he asked. "Mary said Lara's on a trip. You old dog. Been puffing the magic dragon? Bit of the old reefer? Where is it–wouldn't mind a few puffs myself, if you please."

"No, no," Mark said.

Finn looked puzzled.

"Well, thought maybe we'd pop down to the End of the Road to have a pint or three. What do you say?"

Mark didn't relish the thought of leaving his image, but he didn't want to be unneighborly. And a few pints would be no problem for his new, fit self.

"Why don't you toss on some clothes?" Finn said, "then meet me in the truck."

The rusty pickup bounced along the dusty road, over

41

potholes, *ga-dunk, ga-dunk, ga-dunk,* to the front door of the pub. Sitting on a barstool next to Finn, Mark happily knocked back two or three pints of heavy stout beer. The thick, creamy foam on top tickled his lips the way his toes tickled on the den rug when he was naked. He had looked too thin in the mirror. He needed to mitigate the bad effects of years of too much exercise, too much healthy eating. He ordered another beer, and a platter of fried onion rings.

On the way home, Finn's truck *ga-dunked* so hard over one particularly deep pothole, the passenger side visor slipped down, revealing a small vanity mirror inset into the vinyl. Mark squinted at the mirror. The same old man from the mirror at Mom's Diner peered back at him. This can't be right.

"Can't you go faster?" Mark said.

"What's the hurry? Mary said Lara's away for a month."

"I need to get home," Mark said.

Mark dashed through the den door, stripped his clothes off in a flash, then bounded to the mirror. He looked more beautiful, more fit, than ever in the glass. He was alright. Perfect. Finn really ought to dump that old beater and get a proper truck, with good mirrors. What's wrong with people? First the diner, then Finn.

Mark decided to spend some time alone. Other people just weren't reliable. He emailed his office assistant, asking her to reschedule his appointments for a month. He didn't want to see his patients. Mrs. Bernstein's Botox injections for her crow's feet would have to wait. Ms. Kantor's lip filler, too. These treatments, so temporary. The glycolic acid skin peels didn't make Margie Freeman younger. Morty Mehi's liposuction wouldn't bring back his lost vitality. So depressing, these patients. They were iris stalks whose blooms had withered. They looked to Mark to restore their youth, to smooth over this, to plump up that, in a futile effort to deny that age, wrinkles, dissolution, and death lurked just around the corner.

The next morning, Mark showered in the upstairs bathroom, then brushed his teeth. He had covered the mirror over the bathroom sink a few days earlier, as it had appeared to be faulty. He had also slipped Lara's handheld mirror into the bathroom drawer. That just left the mirror in the den, which he knew he could rely upon. He put on his bathrobe and slippers and paddled down to the den. There, he made his plan for the rest of the month. He would eat out, breakfast, lunch, and dinner, every day while Lara was away. This would allow him to reconnect with all his favorite restaurants from before he converted to Lara's vegetarian diet a few years ago. He needed to add a few pounds on. He started this morning once again at Mom's Diner.

"What'll it be, Doctor E?" the waitress asked. Her mother was a regular glycolic acid peel patient.

"Oh," Mark said, "just the Belgian waffle, home fries,

two eggs with cheese, and coffee."

"That it, Doc?"

"Well, how are the blueberry pancakes today?"

After gobbling it all up with alarming speed, Mark went to the rest room. He scrubbed his hands in the sink, dried them with the air dryer, then took a small screwdriver from his front pocket and proceeded to remove the little mirror from the wall over the sink, without looking into the glass. He slipped the mirror through the slot atop the bathroom wastebasket.

"There," he said, "problem solved."

For lunch, Mark stuffed a stuffed pizza in his face, at Heavenly Pizza. For supper, he ingurgitated an entire meatloaf at Moe's, along with a side of mashed potatoes with gravy. Then he mowed through an enormous bowl of pistachio ice cream at his favorite ice cream parlor. He thought, perhaps, he should balance his new diet a bit, so he drove to Humphry Yogurt, where he guzzled two blueberry smoothies.

He parked the truck at home, entered the den, removed all his clothes, and shuffled to the mirror. There he was, this beautiful man, rosier cheeked and slimmer than the day before. He looked more remarkable than ever.

The rest of the month, Mark kept to his plan, visiting every eatery, diner, café, fine restaurant, hole–in–the–

wall, dive bar, even the food counter at the bowling alley. At the close of each day, he stood in front of the den mirror, as naked as on the day of his birth, but even more exquisite. Then the next day, he was at it again, gobbling, gorging, gulping, guzzling, slopping, sloshing, stuffing, even swallowing whole, every food and drink imaginable. He Hoovered the hamburgers at Harry's, he bolted the bisque at Chowder House, he scarfed the pastrami sandwich at Howie's Deli. For balance, he also wolfed down the wedge salad at Veggie Palace.

The more Mark consumed, the more remarkable he looked in the mirror. He had discovered one of life's great mysteries: that gluttony and indolence, at least for Doctor Mark E. Glassman, were the keys to eternal beauty.

Mark was naked in front of the mirror one night, preening and parading as he soaked up the view, when he heard shattering glass. He turned to see Lara staring at him, a bowl from Uganda in pieces by her feet.

"Mark, my God, what happened to you?" Lara cried.

"I'm not sure," Mark said, "I feel great. Just look at me!" he said, gazing again at his image in the mirror. "I've never looked this good, have I? Even more remarkable than before you left. Take off your clothes, Lara, look in the mirror!"

Lara looked at Mark. He appeared fifteen or even twenty pounds heavier than before her trip. His bloated face more sallow, more pitted; his sagging stomach alarmingly swollen.

"Mark, Mark, my God!"

Mark looked in the mirror. He was so beautiful he began to cry.

AVRAM'S MIRACLE

Nearly shouting, to be heard over the cacophony in the vast building, Avram Kantor, the apprentice baker, reported, "There are two men to see you, Rabbi."

Avram and the Rabbi stood in the middle of the largest matzah bakery in the world, the A. Rubinstein & Co. factory, in Cincinnati, Ohio.

"Two men," said Rabbi Rubinstein, stroking his beard with one hand while holding up two fingers with the other. "Two men. You know these men?"

"I do not, Rabbi," Avram shouted, confident that the strangers, seated far away in the lobby of the bakery, would not hear. The plant was buzzing with the hubbub of nearly two hundred bustling bakers and their apprentices. The air was filled with a great din, from the maze of commercial machines to roll, knead, perforate, and cut dough; from giant automated packaging equipment; from whirring dishwashers; from humming refrigerators and freezers; and from a myriad of rolling carts being whisked this way and that with dizzying precision.

"You say you do not know these men," the Rabbi noted, still stroking his long beard. "Yet you say they are here to see me."

Avram nodded earnestly. He was a fine, handsome,

lanky young man, with a pale complexion, Paul Newman-blue eyes, and curly hair so thick and golden it looked as if a bushel of sun-kissed marigolds had sprouted on his head and grown out since birth. For this, he and his parents were mercilessly teased in Avram's early years. Questions about whether Avram was a Kantor naturally led him to wonder if he had been adopted. And, if so, was he Jewish?

Avram found rules impossible. Impossible to understand. Impossible to follow, except for the rules he made. "You're as Jewish as you want to be," was a new rule he decided one day. He determinedly announced this new rule whenever someone questioned his origins. Still, the painful pestering persisted, especially as his parents and three sisters were of dark hair and eyes.

"Where did you get that one?" Uncle Morris once said to his mother, looking at Avram, as Morris tipped a full highball tumbler to his lips at the basement bar of Avram's parents' house, sloshing the mixture of whiskey, ginger ale, and carbonated water onto the wooden bar, much to the annoyance of Avram's teetotaler mother, Sadie.

"Better keep an eye on Sadie" Aunt Millie whispered with a wink to Avram's father, Ruben, the chemist, who was mixing concoctions with a chemist's precision behind his bar, after she had sipped one too many of Ruben's Pink Ladies at a shiva for their dear friend, the deceased local bookie.

Even Ruben's brother, a cantor in the nearby synagogue, chimed in. "I know you're a man of science, Ruben," he had said, "and I'm just Cantor Kantor, but it does seem odd—Avram looks more Swedish than Jewish. Is there something you want to tell me?"

Sloshing a highball at the Kantor's home bar, at yet another shiva, this one for their dear friend, the local fruit peddler, who died in a tragic fruit cart mishap, Howie the Butcher chortled, "are you sure he's one of *us*?" to Ruben, who, despite his passion for logic and science, and his generally gentle disposition, and his years of marching for civil rights and pacifism, removed the thick spectacles from his face, and then promptly punched out Howie's lights. The one and only punch Ruben had thrown in his life, albeit with uncanny, scientific precision. After this unseemly thwacking—for which Ruben was eternally remorseful—there was from time to time, for many subsequent months, a delivery boy from Howie's Deli delivering free brisket, potato knishes, or roast chicken to the Kantor's front door.

"Two men?" the Rabbi asked again, now wiggling the two fingers he still held aloft.

"Yes, Rabbi."

"They may well be men," the Rabbi said, "yet, when is a man, who is a man, not a man?"

"I'm not sure," Avram confessed. Avram thought the Rabbi possessed great wisdom, though he often found the Rabbi more confusing than rules.

49

"When he is a bill collector," the Rabbi explained. "Do these men have the appearance of bill collectors?"

"No, Rabbi. One said he is from Kreigman's."

"Come, Avram, let us meet these men."

Normally, an apprentice would not participate in such a meeting. But the Rabbi was rather fond of Avram, and he knew Avram took an interest in his daughter, Sosha.

Despite its dominance in the powerful global matzah market, A. Rubinstein & Co. was struggling. Cash was short due to the recent expansion of the factory, a move the Rabbi made to compete with a well-financed, upstart competitor, V. Horowitz Kosher Foods, in Poughkeepsie. Horowitz's location in New York meant lower costs for delivering matzah to the lucrative New York and New Jersey metropolitan matzah markets. The Rabbi responded with a plant expansion aimed first at increasing production from the existing facility in Ohio, with plans to later open a new factory in the northeast. The Rabbi was going to give these matzah mogul wannabees a run for their matzah money. And he had another card up his sleeve. His ace-in-the-hole: Kreigman's.

Kreigman's, based in Cincinnati, was the largest grocery chain in the United States. The Rabbi had called Moses Kreigman, the owner, a few days earlier, as well as calling the owner of the largest flour miller in the country. He was going to ask Moses to lead him to the promised land of mass matzah distribution, and the miller, Levi Smalls, to supply the great quantity of flour which would be needed for worldwide matzah domination.

In the lobby, the Rabbi and Avram shook hands with Moses Kreigman, a tall, imposing, serious man in a dark suit, who introduced them to another imposing, serious, dark-suited man, Levi Smalls, the owner of General Smalls Mills, the biggest flour miller in America. The three titans and Avram walked into the conference room immediately off the lobby. There, the Rabbi explained his vision for the three companies to coordinate plans to create a global matzah dynasty. Kreigman's would sell only Rubinstein's matzah, and the vast demand for flour would be met by Smalls's big flour mills. The three would establish a new company and share in the profits. They all agreed, then Levi and Moses asked for a tour.

Part way through the factory, Moses, a man of great curiosity, cracked open the door to a diminutive room the group was walking past.

"What's this?" he asked.

The room was empty, except for a large, heavy wooden table in the middle. On the table was something strange. It was an array of equipment which appeared to be scientific. On one end, a large, circular, clear plastic barrel, with concentric glass tubes inside, spun slowly. The barrel was connected with more clear tubes to glass beakers, to glass globes with rubber stoppers on top, and to more, wider tubes, at the opposite end of the table. The rotating barrel was affixed somehow to gears beneath, which in turn were connected by wires to a large lead acid battery. Liquid inside the contraption periodically bubbled, burbled, then belched through escape vents.

"Well," the Rabbi said, slipping between Levi and Moses to press his face closer to the mysterious contraption, "it's clearly a, yes, clearly–Gideon, come here!"

Avram left hurriedly to find Gideon, the head baker, who was on the factory floor. A few moments later, Avram re-appeared with Gideon, who squeezed between the men to get close to the mysterious machine.

"Gideon," the Rabbi said, "will you please explain to our guests the function of this device?"

Gideon bent over, stuck his spectacled face next to the turning barrel. Then he jumped back, having been startled when the mysterious machine emitted another series of burbly belches.

"Well, Gideon, we are waiting."

"Yes, Rabbi," said Gideon, weakly, "it's clearly a, clearly, yes, a *device*, which, of course, is meant for a *purpose*."

The Rabbi nodded.

"Gentlemen, please, if you will," the Rabbi said, "let us continue our tour. Gideon, take that foolish toy apart." The men headed to the door.

"Wait!" shouted Avram.

"Avram," the Rabbi said, "what is the meaning of this?"

"It's mine, you see. I invented it," Avram said.

"There you are!" exclaimed Sosha, darting her head into the little room. "I've been looking all over for you, Father. Oh, hello, Avram! Goodness, what's that?" she added, catching sight of the mysterious contraption. Sosha was tall, lithe, with long brunette hair, large hazel eyes, and a pretty smile. All the men except the Rabbi and Avram straightened their posture, took air into their lungs, and cleared their throats, the way older men often do when an attractive woman enters.

"Well, you see, Rabbi" Avram began to explain, "it's my invention."

"What does it do, Avram?" the Rabbi asked.

"I didn't say anything because I couldn't be sure it would work, you see. But finally, just this morning, after I made further adjustments to the polymer strands, it began working. It works, you see," he said, then cackled with the excitement of a chicken which has just laid its first egg.

"Excellent!" declared the Rabbi. "It does–what?"

"Well, it's rather scientific, Rabbi."

"I can see that."

"It has to do with chemistry."

"Yes, Avram, but what does it *do*?"

"Well, of course you know what wheat is. Well, you may not have realized that the chemical composition of wheat contains cellulose and pentosans, polymers based on xylose and arabinose, which are, of course, tightly bound proteins. The machine unbinds these, and then, through the reformulation of polymers present in the cell walls, produces self-generating proteins and carbohydrates. It's rather simple, really."

"In English, Avram!" the Rabbi shouted.

"It makes wheat," Avram said.

All in the room looked gobsmacked.

"It's impossible," everyone in the room scoffed.

"No, actually, it is possible, quite possible," Avram said cheerily, "just add water here," he noted, pointing to a spigot on the wheat making machine. "You can make an endless supply of wheat. With enough machines—I'd say forty or fifty—you can produce enough wheat for the entire matzah market. We can feed the world, actually. I've already made a box of matzah using this wheat."

"Oh, Avram!" Sosha shouted, "you've done it! You'll be worshipped, a hero. Everyone will love you!" She flung her arms around Avram's shoulders and kissed him—for the first time—squarely on the lips.

"Sosha!" the Rabbi stammered.

"But Father, isn't it marvelous? Avram's done it. Now people all over the world will be able to eat–*for free.*"

The Rabbi smiled broadly. This could be one of the greatest inventions in history. Levi and Moses looked grim.

That night, to celebrate Avram's new triumph, Avram and Sosha went out for Chinese food with their good friends, Hannah and Ray. They told them the whole story.

"Isn't it marvelous?" Sosha asked at the end of the story, holding her wine glass up for the others to clink in celebration. "Soon no one will ever be hungry again, and Avram will be loved the world over."

"They'll never let you get away with it," Hannah said.

"Whatever do you mean?" Sosha asked.

"Feeding people for free. They won't let it happen," Hannah said. "I'm sorry, Sosha, Avram, but as a businessperson, I know your invention is a threat."

"That's right," Ray said, "I'm just a painter—more interested in pointillism than polymers—but I read about a car some guy invented that will go a thousand miles on one gallon of gas, and of course it never got to market. They bury such things, don't they?"

Avram and Sosha looked at each other pensively.

"Where's that blasted tea?" the Rabbi cried the next morning in his conference room. Levi and Moses sat across from him, glumly ruminating. The Rabbi stood, picked up the conference room phone, and dialed.

"Asher," Levi said, to the Rabbi, "we need a plan."

The Rabbi, still standing, placed the handset back on the receiver.

"The way I see it, we have to act now," Levi said. "We must dispose of this invention before it disposes us."

"But Sosha is right, Levi," the Rabbi said. "Avram's machine will change the world. Progress! Millions of people across the globe no longer need to go hungry. This could be the greatest invention since wheat. Not just for matzah. We can give the world an endless supply of any wheat product, of say–bagels."

"People will have bagels, and that is good," said Moses, speaking calmly and softly.

"Yes," the Rabbi said.

"What of the farmers?" Moses said.

"They can have free bagels, too," the Rabbi said.

"But what of their farms, what of their jobs?" Moses said. "There'll be no wheat to grow. What of the workers the farmers employ? What of the companies that make the tractors and the harvesters?"

"And the fertilizer manufacturers?" Levi said. "And the companies that make farm clothing. One industry after another, gone overnight. This machine is not heaven sent, Asher. It's from the Devil. It's the Devil's matzah! It's going to make us all poor. It's Communism, I say, Communism, that's what it is."

"That's right, Asher," Moses said, "it will be the end of civilization as we know it. This boy, Avram, oh, I'm sure he means well, but we can't be running around giving away food. It will upset the natural order. It's against God, Rabbi, if I may respectfully suggest. After all, did not God command that man must work for his daily bread?"

"Yes, I see now," said the Rabbi, plopping back dejectedly into his chair. "But what can we do?"

"We can buy it from Avram," Moses said, "then destroy it."

The Rabbi picked up the phone handset again. "Mildred, have Avram sent to the conference room at once."

The three men spoke desultorily while they waited. Wasn't it a bit chilly this morning? Isn't that an interesting houndstooth pattern on the Rabbi's new suit? Can you believe the price of tea these days? A few minutes later, all three were hovering over Avram, who was seated at the conference room table. Moses slipped a white envelope onto the table, just under Avram's nose.

"What's this?" Avram asked.

"We think your invention is brilliant," Moses said. Avram beamed. "We'd like to buy it, Avram," Moses said. "You're young, after all, an inventor, no need to trouble yourself with the mundane details of business. We'll handle all of that for you."

"Splendid!" Avram said. "And then you'll use it to feed the world."

"Avram," the Rabbi said quietly, placing a hand on one of Avram's shoulders, "we don't want to bring the machine into production."

"But what do you mean?" Avram asked, confused.

"Think of the farmers," the Rabbi said.

"And the farm workers," Levi said.

"And the companies that make farm equipment, and fertilizers, and farm clothes, and tools–a host of industries. What's to become of the thousands of workers–the tens of thousands–that will be put out of work?" Moses said. "What of them, of their livelihoods, of their families?"

"We can't have Communism, Avram," Levi said, "we're not in Sweden."

"We must think of the people," Moses said.

Avram's face tightened. "Oh, I see" he whispered.

"Look inside the envelope," Moses said. "There's a signed I.O.U. in there, enough to make you a rich man. You'll be set for life."

"Yes," the Rabbi agreed. "You and Sosha."

"I see," Avram murmured.

Moses handed a pen to Avram.

"Just sign your name in agreement, and you'll never have another worry. You'll be comfortable for the rest of your life."

Avram took the pen from Moses's hand. He slid the I.O.U. out from the envelope and was startled to read the seven-figure number written on it. Avram had never dreamt of such a sum. He moved the pen to the paper. As he began to sign his name, his eyes closed, and he suddenly glimpsed into his future. He saw a large, cozy farmhouse, with a white picket fence, and little children darting about the fields. There was Sosha, standing on the farmer's porch, as beautiful as ever, beckoning for him to come in and warm himself by the fire. He felt the chill, thin air on his cheeks, heard twigs snapping under his fine leather boots as he strode towards his beloved, and he smelled sweet-sour autumnal apples decomposing atop beds of musty leaves. He sighed contentedly while his hand began moving the pen to form the letters of his name.

Then, in his reverie, something changed. Weary, gray, gaunt faces of men, women and children in tattered clothing appeared, pressing in from the edges of his dreamscape. First a few, then a few dozen, then hundreds—thousands. They were poor; they were hungry. They pressed in closer and closer to the farm, thousands, millions of starving, lost souls. They stretched open their mouths to scream for help, but they had no voices. As they pressed in ever closer, Avram's face grew dark. His wild eyes shot open. He bolted up from the chair, flung the pen across the room, then momentarily froze—as motionless as Lot's wife who, after disobeying God and looking back at the destruction of Sodom, was turned into a pillar of salt.

"No, I shall not sign," Avram whispered. "You're all mad!" he cried, then he dashed out through the conference room doors.

"What should we do," the Rabbi asked, looking at the other two men.

"Either we destroy that machine," Moses said, "or we destroy that man—before he destroys us."

"God Lord, Moses, I can never condone violence," the Rabbi said.

"You'll have violence when millions lose their livelihoods."

"So, what should we do?" the Rabbi said.

"We should offer more money," Levi said.

"Avram doesn't care about money," the Rabbi said, "he's young, he hasn't a care in the world."

"He cares about Sosha," Moses said.

The Rabbi sighed, slowly nodding his head.

That night, the Rabbi knocked lightly on Sosha's bedroom door.

"So, you see, Sosha," he whispered gently, sitting on the edge of the bed and holding her hands, "we just want you to talk to Avram. To talk some sense into him. He's a dreamer, but he appears not to grasp that his dream will put millions out of work. He'll listen to you, Sosha."

"I see, Father. So, you want to offer me up, is that it?"

"No, Sosha, I just want to help the people."

"Which people, Father?"

"You've never been poor, Sosha. It wouldn't suit you."

The next day, Sosha met Avram at the factory with a picnic lunch. They strolled to a nearby park. Together they spread out a blanket on the grass, then put out food and drinks, along with the box of magic machine matzah Avram brought. Matzah made with the wheat from his new miracle. It was a fine, crisp, sunny fall day. As Avram began to eat, Sosha caressed his hand.

"Avram," Sosha said, "Father told me he wants to purchase your invention."

Avram placed the sandwich on the napkin.

"He said you'll be a rich man."

Avram scowled. "He doesn't want to use my invention. It's all I have."

"You'd have me, Avram," she trilled, caressing his arm.

"Oh, Sosha!" he cried, hugging her hard. They had been dating only awhile, and Avram now confessed his love. Then he hugged Sosha even harder, eyes closed, tears of joy on his cheeks. Then, eyes still shut, he glimpsed the future again. The farmhouse, lovely Sosha beckoning him in, little ones scampering about, all safely behind a tidy white picket fence. Then they appeared once more—the hundreds, the thousands of gray, gaunt, starving people, stretching their mouths open wide in silent screams.

"I can't take their money," Avram said.

"Not even for me?" Sosha said.

"I'm sorry, Sosha. Not even for you. Not even for love. Some things are bigger than just two people."

"Oh, Avram!" she said, suddenly jumping up from the blanket. "Thank God!"

"What do you mean?"

"If you told me you would take the money, I would never speak to you again. Let's go tell Father the news. Then we can go to the newspapers—we can show them everything. The box of matzah, your diagrams of the machine. They can tell the world!"

When they walked back to the factory, they were surprised to see a large crowd gathered in front. Men and women in overalls, plaid shirts, and boots, some with pitchforks and rakes and shovels. Avram held Sosha's hand tightly while clutching the box of miracle matzah under his arm. They stood in front of the crowd, of hundreds of people, at a distance.

Earlier that morning, Moses had called the local farm workers union to tell them of the new machine and of the danger to their livelihoods.

"What's this, then?" Avram shouted.

"We want our jobs!" one man shouted at Avram.

"If you feed everyone, what will we do?" said another.

"We need to work," a woman said.

"We don't want you Communists here! Go back to Sweden!"

Sosha feared for Avram. She held her arms out wide as if to try to block the swelling crowd, as men and women were stepping forward toward her and Avram.

"They just want me," Avram whispered to her.

And with that, he was off, dashing madly away from the crowd, which began chasing him at full tilt. He scampered over a chain link fence into a maze of alleyways and side streets. He heard the thuds of boots on asphalt but, glancing behind, saw no one. He ran on, wildly, his long legs keeping him ahead of the chase, all the while still clutching the box of magic matzah. He ran on and on, having been quite fleet on his feet for his whole life. The angry mob kept up the chase, sometimes gaining on him a bit, but then Avram would again pull ahead.

As he rounded the corner past Daniela's Violin Studio, on Exodus Street, he slowed momentarily to listen to the maestro's sweet strains of Mendelsohn's concerto wafting through her open windows. Then he raced on. He may have got away, too, had it not been for the good bit of dog poo which the maestro's poodle had deposited at the far end of the street.

When the crowd got up to him, Avram was lying on his back in the street. The crowd stopped running and began walking toward him slowly. He thought he was in for a beating—or worse. The box of matzah was on the asphalt next to him. He stood up slowly, the matzah box in hand.

Avram faced the crowd of men and women with clenched fists, and tight, angry faces.

"I, I just wanted to help people," Avram stammered.

The crowd was silent, moving towards him.

"I wanted to feed people. That's all. See."

Avram opened the top of the matzah box in order to remove a large square matzah to show the crowd. But his face took on a strange, puzzled expression when his hand entered the box. His fingers felt only crumbs, a thousand minuscule crumbs. Avram turned the box upside down and shook it. A dust cloud of matzah crumbs fell from the box and blew away with a bit of wind. Avram looked in the box—it was empty.

The cloud of matzah dust swirled toward the crowd and then evaporated. Everyone paused, then began to laugh.

"It's just dust," someone hollered. "All dust."

"It's a fraud, it doesn't work, there's no miracle!" another said.

"Our jobs are saved!"

The crowd began to disperse, leaving Avram slowly shaking the upside-down matzah box in disbelief.

"The molecules are unstable," Avram muttered, "causing faulty reformulation of the polymers. I only need to adjust the self-generation of proteins and carbohydrates to enhance the stability." He smiled, knowing this was an easy fix.

The next morning, Avram met Sosha at the train station. They were leaving together. They hugged and kissed inside the terminal, waiting to elope, waiting for the train that would take them to their new life.

Moses and Levi had smashed the miracle matzah machine to smithereens. But no matter. Avram smiled as he patted the coat pocket in which he had the original lab notes and plans for the machine, as well as the modifications he had noted to ensure the stability of the wheat the machine would produce. He would use the notes to make a new, even better machine. In revising the design, he had a God-given epiphany. He told Sosha about it now while they embraced.

"Not only wheat," he whispered to Sosha. "We can invent machines that will make corn, rice, and barley."

"Oh, Avram," Sosha exclaimed, "the world is going to love you!"

THE BOX

Head bowed, lost in her hefty, hardcover, first edition of *The Virgin Warrior, The Life and Death of Joan of Arc,* Francine was so entranced by the story of Joan's divine inspiration–not to mention of Joan refusing to wear "feminine clothes" and to pursue the "avocations of women"–she didn't notice her plate of vegetarian vindaloo had gone cold. She had dunked the flat bottom of one of the spiced potato samosa triangles in the vindaloo six chapters ago, then forgotten it in the liquid. As she read of Joan toppling the English at their failed siege of Orléans, the samosa, its once firm crust having absorbed more liquid than any samosa could bear, finally lost The Battle of Vindaloo. It toppled over in a mushy mess, spilling its contents from its side, split like an English soldier gutted by a sword-thrust of cold French steel.

"For you," a soft voice–nearly a whisper–said.

Francine looked up at the young woman standing by her table at India Restaurant. Though beautiful, she had a pained look on her face. A turquoise head scarf, tied in a bow on one side, covered her hair. From her shoulders, a dark burgundy sari draped along the length of her body like a shimmering curtain of blood. She was adorned with silver and gold rings, bangles, bracelets, and a paper-thin silver nose ring. She sat hurriedly in the chair opposite Francine. As Francine was about to ask if they knew each other, the sylphlike stranger silently placed a box, about the size of Francine's book, between them on the table, next to Francine's cell phone. Francine stared at the many gold and silver rings on the woman's slender brown fingers, as she slid the box closer to her. The box had dark wooden sides, a glass top, and a gold clasp in the shape of a cross in front.

"For happiness," the woman said.

"I'm sorry," Francine said, "do we know each other– maybe from the University? Did you take one of my art classes?"

The woman quickly stood up, then walked briskly out of India. Francine watched her go through the front window–a glimmering shard of turquoise and burgundy flaming out beneath the summer sun.

How strange! Francine ran her fingers along the sides of the box. The smooth dark wood felt surprisingly cold. She opened the clasp, lifted the lid: the box was empty. So dark was the wood inside, perhaps of an ebony or African Blackwood, Francine was not sure she could see the bottom. She felt a chill, then closed the box, and in so doing, when some of her fingers pressed on the glass top, the glass lit up. Then, there it was, in the glass, a picture of Avery, her dinner date for tonight. She recognized it as the same picture she had saved on her phone, a screenshot from his dating profile. This must be some new digital picture frame college kids are using. Must somehow sync with my cell phone photos. But who was the young woman? And why this box? A gift from a shy former student? Francine gathered her belongings, slipped the box into her tote bag, next to *The Virgin Warrior*, paid the bill, and walked home. She wanted time to finish the sketch of Avery's face before dinner with him. At home, she placed the box on the living room coffee table, next to the easel, on which she then finished the sketch.

She had met Avery on a dating app, *Plenty of Fish*, the week before. She'd thought it was a stupid name for a lame idea–online dating.

"It works, Francie, you should try it," her sister Mary had said on the phone. "No, Phil, for *Christ's* sake," Mary hollered, "how should I know where your head razor is?"

"I want to meet someone in real life, Mary, like we did in college–not on a computer," Francine said. She was sitting in bed, in navy blue satin pajama bottoms, and a white satin top, sipping Bordeaux, while her cat, Souris, purred on her lap.

"Hello, Francie," Mary said, "this is the nineties calling: we've come to take our dating back."

"Very funny," Francine said.

"You've got to get with the times, Sis," Mary said, "I mean, that's how people meet these days. That's how Phil and I met, and we're happy."

"Are you?" Francine said. "Are you happy?"

"Yes, of course," Mary said. "Oh, sometimes Phil acts like a head in a jar–men do that–and he doesn't talk much, at least not about feelings–they don't do that, do they?–still, we're happy, we're always happy. We'll always be happy. Christ, Phil, I already told you, I can't help you look for it now, I'm on the phone."

"I don't know, Mary," Francine said, "where's the romance?" She lifted the wine to her lips, and sipped, holding the goblet there, as she ran the tip of her tongue along the lower rim of the cool glass.

"Just try it, Francie. You just look at pics, then swipe left if you don't like them. Easy-peasy! It's not like I'm asking you to be burned at the stake, for Christ's sake."

"Who else would I be burned at the stake for?" Francine said.

"Huh?" Mary said.

"I said, who else–"

"You can be so hard to figure, Francie. You're not *seeing* things again, are you?"

"I'm fine," Francine said.

"Because if you're seeing things," Mary said, "I can take you to that doctor what's-his-name."

"I'm fine, Mary. I don't have visions, like Joan of Arc. It's just Synesthesia. I see colors in things, like music. I don't hear voices. No visions sent by God."

"Well, still, you can't just live with your cat. A woman can't just live with her cat. I still don't get why you named it in French for *mouse*. It's a little weird, Sis. Men don't like that."

"Don't like cats?" Francine said.

"Weird," Mary said, "men don't like weird."

"I'm fine, Mary, and I don't need a man."

"Yes, but wouldn't a man be *better*?"

"Better than what?" Francine said.

"Better than a mouse. For Christ's sake, I *said* I'll come help find your head razor. You'd *lose* your head if it wasn't screwed on, Phil. Maybe you should just keep it in a jar. No, Phil, not your razor, your *head*. Yes, in a *jar*. You're not listening, Phil, are you? You never listen. You're going to drive me to drink. I've got to go, Francie, sorry. Try the app, OK? I'm worried about you, Sis, alone with a cat. I just want you to be happy."

A few nights later, in her loft apartment in the City, in bed, with Souris on her lap, Francine clicked on the App Store on her phone. She downloaded *Plenty of Fish*. Why not have a look? I don't need a man, but it will make Mary happy if I say I looked. She filled out the registration online; entered her credit card information; set up her profile. That was the hard part. The app wanted to know who she was.

Who am I? I'm a strong, fierce feminist, who doesn't

71

need–. No, no, strike that–that's no good. ~~Who am I? I'm a strong, fierce, feminist, who doesn't need–~~.

Who am I? I'm a well-adjusted woman whose unhappy sister won't stop nagging her about–. ~~Who am I? I'm a well-adjusted woman whose unhappy sister won't stop nagging her about–~~.

Who am I? I'm an independent, college educated artist and academic, living a rich, full life, surrounded by loving family, and amazing friends. ~~Most nights, I prefer to be alone with my cat, painting or reading~~. Most nights, I prefer to be alone with my cat, painting or reading. My life has been rich with travel and other experiences. I'm satisfied. But lately, I've begun to realize having someone to share ~~life's adventures, life's journeys, life's challenges~~, life with, would be ~~agreeable, acceptable~~, rewarding. ~~After all,~~ I'm already thirty-five, ~~and Joan of Arc was put to death at just nineteen~~, and ready ~~although, as the French say, il vaut mieux être seul que mal accompagné, which means it is better to be alone than in bad company~~ for a life of joie de vivre. ~~Must love cats. No drugs. Please don't be an asshole~~. Yes, that's it:

Who am I? I'm an independent, college educated artist and academic, living a rich, full life, surrounded by loving family, and amazing friends. My life has been rich with travel and other experiences. I'm satisfied. But lately, I've begun to realize having someone to share life with would be rewarding. I'm already thirty-five, and ready for a life of joie de vivre.

She posted a photo of herself, clicked Save, then, within minutes, her phone pinged with her first bite. Oh, no, no, not that one. She swiped left to make the grizzled man in a plaid flannel shirt, sitting on the hood of his red pickup truck, flashing a yellow smile, disappear. Then she swiped left, left, left on her cell phone, one picture after another, swiping with ever-increasing rapidity. Swiping past men kissing fish; men clutching rifles; men gripping antlers. Oh, my, she muttered, at the image of a man kissing a fish bigger than Souris. Gross, she hissed, at a man carrying what might have been an elephant gun, without, thank Heaven, an elephant in view. *Ew*, she said, at a man holding deer antlers which were, horrifying, attached to the head of a deer. She began swiping so fast her eyes could barely process the image of one foul man before the next, fouler one appeared. Her artist's fingers flying so nimbly, she almost swiped past Avery. She caught herself just in time, her right index fingertip already feathering the phone screen, starting another leftward *swoosh*. She froze just before it was too late, as Avery's delicate features, soft brown eyes–an undefinable sweetness–came into view. Something about his image so caught her, she pressed the two side buttons on her phone to take a screen shot of his face.

She read the profile below his picture. It spoke of his love of poetry, café culture, black and white movies, and witty repartee. At last, a man of some refinement. And a young college professor, to boot. She clicked REEL IN on the stupid app, just below his picture. Within a minute, he clicked, too! Another ping, then a message–IT'S A CATCH–scrolled across her phone screen. Who writes these dumb phrases, anyway?

After "reeling in" each other, they texted through the app for a few days, finally arranging for a phone call. Avery had a kind, baritone voice; a soft, English accent. He taught fifteenth century English poetry, and had just started a position that semester, at the University. Before the call ended, they arranged for Sunday dinner at his apartment. She was surprised she had allowed herself to move so quickly. But she felt that she knew Avery. He, too, lived in the City, not far from her, close enough for her to walk.

That's where she walked the evening after receiving the box in India, then finishing the sketch at home. She put on a pair of black bootcut jeans, black army boots, and a men's gray dress shirt. She liked the feel of the soft cotton, and the looseness of the cut, which afforded a freedom of movement missing in women's clothes, which, she was sure, were designed by men. She pulled her short black hair, just long enough for a small ponytail, behind her, and tied a fancy white hair elastic. She put her sketch of Avery between pages of the Joan of Arc book, slipped the book into her tote, then locked the front door behind her. Although she didn't need a man–I'm just fine, I don't need anyone–as she weaved her way along the City sidewalks, beneath lustrous, green, leafy oak trees, and the occasional clump of white birches, twisting toward the Heavens like angels' wings, she imagined a future of long walks with a contemplative companion, and, even further out, of nights reading books together by a cozy fireplace. She thought her heart might burst.

Avery's apartment was on the ground floor of a brownstone in a tony neighborhood of the City. "Come in, it's open," a warm baritone voice shouted as soon as the brass door knocker clanged down like a hammer on an anvil. She opened the heavy door, said, "hello, it's Francine," and when a voice from another room replied "welcome," she entered the rest of the way, closing the door behind her. An elderly man appeared at the end of the dim hallway. He had Avery's nose, cheeks, and eyes, but appeared to be twice her age. It's strange that Avery didn't mention his father would be home when she arrived.

"Welcome, Francine," the man said, in his warm, baritone voice. "I'm Avery."

In a flash, Francine saw all the oak leaves wither, then flutter to the ground, gathering in cold, musty, dead clumps. The birches, blown in a winter gale, bent, broke, then toppled. Logs in the cozy fire of her future burned down to small heaps of smoldering, black ashes.

"Won't you come into the kitchen," Avery said, pointing behind him. "I've baked you a wonderful fish dinner."

Francine looked at him, down the hallway, and wondered how she could reach him. The hallway was brimming with floor to ceiling shelves, bookcases, and storage units of all kinds, each chock-full of shoes, coffee makers, clothes, and assorted knick-knacks. One long shelf was filled with dozens of snow globes. Another with figurines, apparently elves. So full was the space, she would have had to walk sideways to traverse the long distance from the front door to the kitchen.

"I'm a bit of a collector," Avery said. "Especially of shoes. I have fifty pairs of Oxfords. I love them! Also, cappuccino machines, though just thirty-three. I collect those for my birthday. I buy a new machine each year; started when I was thirty. Kind of fun. I love coffee. Well, let's not let the fish get cold. They're bottom feeders, flounders, so they're quite thin, cool quickly."

Francine was unsure what to do. She turned sideways and began to sidle down the hallway, but in a moment, she got stuck, pressed between shelves of elves on one side, and a head-high muddle of shoe storage boxes on the other.

"Oh, I'm terribly sorry," Avery said, "I usually go in and out through the kitchen entrance. Let me see if I can set you free."

He began sidling toward her, and it was then she could see he was not wearing pants. His dress shirt draped below his waist, to where his spindly, pale legs showed. As he moved, the scooped hem of the shirt fluttered up, affording Francine a momentary view of what appeared to be his pink underwear. Avery, catching the expression on Francine's face, said, "they're gym shorts." Francine was unmoved by his explanation, and seeing her unchanged visage, which bore a look of panic tempered by a measure of revulsion, Avery said, "well, if you can't be comfortable in your own home ..."

"Wait!" she shouted. "Please stay there, I think I've got it."

Francine felt a little sorry for Avery. Still, she was angry at him, for his deceit, and at herself, for this predicament.

"I think I can back up," she said.

"Good," he said, "why don't you come round outside to the kitchen door."

The phone rang. "Yes, Mother," Avery said, "of course I'll save some flounder for you if you'll be late for dinner. Yes, she's here, Mother, where else would she be?" But Francine was somewhere else. Having extricated herself from the crush of elves and Oxfords, she had hastened out the front door. She raced along the avenue toward home. She felt foolish and betrayed. There may be plenty of fish, but she didn't want to land one twice her age, and in pink underwear. Not to mention, she'd told him she was a vegetarian, yet, when she arrived for dinner, his apartment reeked of dead flounder. Bottom feeders.

At home, she did what had to be done: she took a long, hot bath. Soaking in the tub, a glass of Bordeaux on the floor next to her, with Souris purring on the countertop while he watched her, she sighed deeply. I don't need a man. I don't need anyone. Mary said she and

Phil are happy, but they're miserable. All happy couples are miserable. Mother and Father had been miserable. Who leaves his daughter when she's eight? He said Mother was "torpid." What kind of man says that to his eight-year-old daughter?

Francine hadn't known what torpid meant, but the abandonment hurt, as sharply as a pin prick. She hated her father, then, and for many years. Until, one day, she didn't. It was strange. As if someone had opened a magic box and released a spell of forgiveness, or as if she awoke, one morning, suddenly grown up, the gnawing hatred having dissolved as completely as a kidney stone in a bath of sodium bicarbonate.

After her bath–in lavender bubbles–resting in her satin pajamas, in the living room, Francine found Avery's picture in her cell phone photo album and deleted it. A strange bluish light glowed from the mysterious box on the coffee table, next to the sofa and the easel. She rose from the sofa, looked down at Avery's picture in the glass top of the box. Maybe his photo appeared in the box because she had just opened his image on her phone so she could delete it. Yes, the box and phone must be connected–somehow. Technology these days! With an index finger, she swiped the glass on top of the box to the left. Avery was gone. Then she remembered the sketch. Her tote bag was on the floor by the sofa. She removed *The Virgin Warrior*, and slid the paper sketch out from the pages. The paper was blank. She turned it over to examine the other side, but there was no sketch of Avery there either. She was tired, it had been an exhausting misadventure, and she'd had a few glasses of wine. I must have placed the wrong sheet of sketch paper in the book. Let's go to bed, Souris. Tomorrow things will be clear.

The next morning, Francine walked to the University. Glancing up occasionally as she walked, she saw that the undersides of the oak tree leaves were covered with slugs, feeding ravenously on the juicy leaves, leaving transparent, skeletonized swaths. Passing a clump of birch trees growing in the postage-stamp front lawn of a townhouse, she noticed long, ugly cankers in the bark, caused by infecting fungi.

"Bonjour, Clarice," she said to the administrative assistant at the College of Art office. She started to ask Clarice to please tell Avery, if he calls, that she is out of her office, but then she realized something: she didn't know Avery's last name.

"I'll be in my office this morning, Clarice, before classes in the afternoon. Will you do me a favor? If a professor from the English Lit Department calls, will you tell him I'm out?"

"Sure thing," Clarice said.

In her office, Francine heaved her tote bag and vegan leather messenger bag onto her desk. She plopped into her desk chair, and sighed, heavily. Am I being too harsh, cutting Avery off like this? It's been ages since I've been out on a date. First dates are always awkward. Still, he was untruthful. But I don't want him to feel badly. Maybe

I'll call and thank him for dinner, make up some excuse for having to leave before the meal. End on a positive note. She dialed his cell phone number but got a message saying this number is out of service. That's odd. They had called each other just days ago. She opened her laptop, went to the University website, then clicked through to the English Literature Department in the University's College of Liberal Arts. She scrolled past the bios and photos of the professors and staff. No one named Avery was listed. Typical–the University was so disorganized; they probably won't have his info online for months. She closed her laptop, took up her cell phone, clicked on the main number for the University in her contacts.

"Thank you for calling the University," a man said, sounding far too happy, then, "every day is an opportunity for education. How may we help you grow today?"

"This is Professor–"

"Hold please."

Francine thought she recognized the theme from *Breakfast at Tiffany's*, although in a sanitized version, suited for an elevator in one of those nameless, nondescript skyscrapers in the City.

"Thank you for calling the University," the happy man said once again, "every day is an opportunity–"

"Yes, I've heard that," Francine said.

"For education–hold please."

"No!" Francine shouted, "I've already heard *Moon River*. I'm just trying to reach a Professor in the English Lit Department." But she was too late.

When the conversation resumed, after another tinny, yet strangely wistful *Moon River*, the man said he did not have a listing for a Professor Avery.

"I'm sorry," Francine said, "Avery is his first name. I don't have his last name."

The man searched. No Avery listed, neither first nor last name.

Francine rolled her eyes as the call ended. The University was so inefficient. Bad enough not to have a new hire on the website, he should at least be in the staff directory. Then she began to grade papers and prepare for afternoon classes.

That night, in another lavender bath, she decided to cancel her trial subscription to *Plenty of Fish*. Careful not to drop her phone into the bath–as she did often–she opened the dating app. Before deleting her own profile, she decided to look at Avery's. Maybe there'd be a clue to his last name. She clicked on the YOUR CATCHES button, but the page was blank. No matter where she clicked in the app, she found no Avery. She and Avery had messaged each other repeatedly, but the messages page, too, was blank.

After the bath, Francine relaxed in her robe, reading more chapters of *The Virgin Warrior*, with Souris next to her on the sofa, and a glass goblet of wine, her cell phone, and the box, next to her on the coffee table. Her phone rang. It was her father, Jules, on a video call. She was startled–they had not spoken in years. She put the book on the table, picked up the wine goblet, took a deep breath, then answered.

"Hello, Francine," Jules said, "it is good to see you. How are things in the City? It is cold here in Paris. But seeing you, I am warmed. I wish you would come to France to visit–it has been so many years! Have you been well? Your face looks chubby, Francine, a little chubby. Are you eating bread? You should not eat bread, or sugar. Best to cut all bread and sugar from your diet, Francine. Well, how have you been? Things are well here, I've been very busy at The Firm, big new project. Let me tell you about my development at the port in Marseille. It's extraordinary. What happened is–"

The conversation continued this way, at great length. After telling Francine in detail about his new project, her father paused a moment, during which Francine hurriedly said, "I've been well, Father. My classes at the University are full, and I'm researching for some new paintings, of Joan of Arc."

"Good, good," Jules said. "That's very good. Now, is there a man?"

"I'm very busy with my career," Francine said.

"Yes, yes," he said, "work is good. Joan of Arc, wonderful, wonderful. But even Joan of Arc deserved some happiness–marriage, children, grandchildren."

"She was burned at the stake when she was nineteen, Father."

"I'm not getting any younger," Jules said. "What about more grandchildren, for me?"

"More grandchildren?" Francine said.

"Didn't Mary tell you? She's pregnant. Twins. She and, um, Phil, yes, Phil, that's it, they'll be so happy with two babies."

Francine's fingers loosened, releasing the goblet of Bordeaux to shatter on the floor.

"Cut out bread, and sugar, Francine," Jules said. "Your mother, God rest her soul, got chubby, it's in the genes, Francine. Chubby ... torpid ... from bread and sugar. Of course, I don't mean to speak ill of the dead. I just want you to be happy."

Francine felt something thick in her throat. Her chest tightened. Feelings long fled flooded in. She remembered her old hatred. Remembered it, then felt it. How it had pricked her like a pin! As Jules babbled on with dated, patriarchal notions, she felt those pins, absent for years, their pricks now sharper, crueler.

"I have to go now," she said, ending the call, and dropping her cell phone on the coffee table, next to the box, which glowed once more with a strange, bluish light. She looked at it, at the top: a picture of her father illuminated in the glass with a faint, cerulean blue. Her hatred and the pin pricks were now so unbearable, she placed a finger on the glass. She held her finger there, wanting but unable to swipe left. She breathed in deeply, exhaled, then cried. She was so lost in the upheaval of emotions, she hadn't even wondered by what strange magic the box had displayed the picture of her father, just when the pinpricks of his callousness became so severe, she had wanted to scream. Still, she had been unable to swipe left.

The next morning, Francine went to see the University Dean about Avery. The Dean had asked her on a date a few years back, but she had nipped that in the bud, and this would simply be a brief meeting of two professionals. She had to know about Avery. She was going to get to the bottom of this.

"You'll need to make an appointment," the Dean's assistant said.

"Please tell him that Francine from the College of Art is here, I just need a few minutes."

"Good to see you, Francine," Hugh Beckett said. He wore the same tweed jacket with the scuffed suede elbow patches he'd worn since she'd first met him years earlier. He stood up, then motioned for her to have a seat in his office.

"How are things. I've heard you're planning on an

exhibit next year?"

"Yes," Francine said. "I'm researching Joan of Arc for the new paintings."

"Ah, Joan of Arc. Didn't end too well for her, did it?" he said, chuckling. She fought the urge to roll her eyes, and to stick the silver letter opener on his desk between his ribs.

"Hugh," she said, "I'm trying to get in touch with a new professor. Teaches English poetry. Name is Avery."

"Doesn't ring a bell," Hugh said. "I'll take a look." He scrolled through the screen on the laptop on his desk. "Nothing here, love. No one by that name. Why do you need to reach him? Do I need to take a number, get in line?"

"Oh, nothing, really. Are you sure?" she said.

Hugh lifted the laptop and walked around his desk to show Francine, still in a chair, that there was no Avery in the directory. As she looked at the screen, he brushed one of her shoulders with the back of his hand, leaned his head down next to her hair, breathed in deeply, then exhaled with a sigh.

"You know, Francine," he said, "you can do great things with your career here at the University. Great things. I can be of service."

"I don't think your wife would approve," Francine said.

"Have dinner with me," he said, "we can work it out."

"What about the wedding ring on your finger?" Francine said. "Can you work that out?"

Hugh stood up, stiffened his back, and said, "I can make things difficult." Then he bent down again and tried to kiss Francine. She was appalled. She wanted to skewer him. She bolted up from the chair and dashed out through the office door.

That night, resting and reading on her sofa, Francine thought about how strange the week had been. The failed date with Avery. The sudden video call with her father. The meeting with Hugh. It was while she reflected upon the meeting with Hugh that the box, next to her cell phone on the coffee table, again emanated a cerulean blue glow. She rose slowly, looked down at the box, saw a picture of Hugh in his grubby sport coat with the suede elbow patches. She couldn't recall having a photo of Hugh in her cell phone. Why would she? If the box just synced with the photos in my phone, how could it display the picture of Hugh? Then, somehow, she knew. Something about this box was not normal, not earthly. Was the box somehow the cause of Avery's vanishment? What if I had swiped left on my father's picture? Would he, too, have evaporated? What would that have meant for Mary, and for me? It was then Francine realized she must cut down. Must drink less wine. Damn, this Bordeaux is good! I hadn't realized how much I've had tonight. Crazy thoughts! From now on, wine only on weekends. She felt like a silly schoolgirl, imaging wild, otherworldly things. Still, she couldn't bear the smug smile on the face of Hugh, in the photo, so she swiped left on the glass, then went to sleep with Souris.

The next morning was sunny and warm. Walking to the University, Francine looked up at the oak trees and saw the slugs had gone. It was a fine day. Every clump of birches she passed appeared pristinely white as new snow. In her office, she used her desk phone to call Hugh. She was sure she could find a way to move forward professionally. He's not a child, after all, not a petulant little boy. She dialed the number for his assistant.

"Dean Pucelle's office, may I help you?" a woman said.

"Oh," Francine said, "I'm calling for Dean Beckett."

"Who?" the woman said. "This is office of the Dean, Catherine Pucelle."

"But that's impossible," Francine said.

Francine placed the handset back on the desk phone cradle without even having said goodbye. She was immobilized, for quite some time. It was not wine. Not her wild imagining. Not her Synesthesia. She remembered the stranger who presented her with the box. How exotic and silent she was. How she disappeared, like a retreating flame flickering out beneath the summer sun. "For happiness," the stranger had said. Francine had been happy. With Souris. With Joan. With her work. With herself. It was others who insisted Francine must be unhappy. Others who wished for her things she did not wish for herself. It was Mary, whose marriage had devolved from early days, of cooing and respect, to sarcasm and resentment. Her father, who wanted grandchildren for posterity, but not a loving family. Mary, Jules, Avery, Hugh—none of them understood her. They only understood their own frustrations and desires.

Francine slipped *The Virgin Warrior,* cell phone, water bottle, pens, pencils, and lesson plans into her tote bag. "I'll be back for afternoon classes, Clarice" she said as she hurried out. At home, she emptied the contents of the tote onto the coffee table, picked up the box with two hands, and placed it into the tote. She locked her door, then walked to India. At the restaurant, she took her usual table.

"Nice to see you today," the waiter said. "I'll get your vegetarian vindaloo. Spicy or mild samosas this time?" he said.

"No, not today, Daksh," Francine said. "Just black tea, thank you."

"No vindaloo?" Daksh said. "Are you feeling alright, Ms. Francine? A woman cannot have just tea. It is not a meal. A woman must eat. She cannot have just tea."

"I'm fine, yes, Daksh," Francine said, "never better. And yes, she can. She can have just tea. She can do as she pleases, Daksh."

Daksh looked puzzled. He went to the kitchen to order the tea.

Francine looked around the restaurant. At the nearest table, an elderly man, sitting alone, was writing on paper, with a fancy pen. Now and then, he held up the paper and read aloud. Francine thought he was writing poetry. He looked–happy. At a further table, a young couple was sharing platters of food–but not eating–on the table between them. They began to argue.

"What about *my* needs?" the man said. "You're always studying. I thought we were going to have a family. You're supposed to take care of me. That's what couples do, isn't it?"

The woman replied, softly. Francine could not hear what she said. The man stood up, then hurriedly left India. The woman began crying. Francine took a sip of tea, placed the cup on the saucer, removed some money from her pocket, and placed it on the table next to the teacup. She picked up the tote, then walked over to the young woman. Francine stood for a moment until the woman looked up at her.

"For you," Francine said. She removed the box from the tote bag, kissed the little golden cross on the front of the box, then placed it on the table. She sat down across from the stranger.

The woman stopped crying. "I'm sorry," she said, "do I know you?"

"For happiness," Francine said. She slid the box closer to the woman. Then she rose quickly and dashed out of India.

THE LONELIEST NUMBER

"Doctor Blume," I whispered, "I'm *tri*polar."

Doctor Blume pursed her lips, leaned back in her brown leather desk chair, removed her horn-rimmed spectacles, and began polishing them with the end of her cornflower blue cashmere cardigan. Then, slowly, deliberately, softly, said, "Well, Irina, what makes you say that?"

I was reclining on a supple, soft, saddle-brown leather couch in Doctor Blume's office on Beacon Street in Boston. It was a cozy, capacious couch. Doctor Blume had diagnosed me two years earlier with "bipolar 2," the type with mild mania, called "hypomania." I knew nothing about bipolar until her diagnosis–which I initially scoffed at ("who, me?"). How dare she call me bipolar, I'd thought. Quack! It's not possible I have a mental illness. I'm just a regular gal. I was angry, bitter. Everyone gets down at times. Everyone has periods of frenetic happiness. Ups, downs, highs, lows. That's normal. That's called normal disorder. What does she expect, my moods to be as flat as a sat-upon pancake? Don't label me as abnormal, as–mentally ill!

But since her diagnosis, I'd read a lot about bipolar disorder. I became a bit of an expert. And I came to understand–and eventually, grudgingly, to agree with– Doctor Blume's diagnosis. It only took two years. For two years after Doctor Blume's initial diagnosis, I continued therapy sessions, but I refused to allow her to insult me with even the mention of bipolar again.

Bipolar people were bad, I thought. They were, well, like, crazy. My first thought, that day Doctor Blume told me in her office I have bipolar disorder, was simply, no fucking way. But over the next two years, I had multiple episodes of deep depression. Although I'd agreed with Dr. Blume to try a bit of medication early on, I kept going off the medication when I felt fine. But eventually I started to sense something was wrong. My highs were moderate, when I happy go-luckily waltzed through life, as light as Audrey Hepburn's Holly Golightly, the free spirit from Tulip, Texas, in *Breakfast at Tiffany's*. But at the end of each high stood the tallest cliff on earth. And on the other side of that cliff was the deepest, blackest hole. Some days, simply trying to get out of bed, get dressed, and propel my limp, deadweight body to Doctor Blume's office felt like Sisyphus trying to push his boulder up, up, up a hill from the deepest depths of Hades. The hole was too black, too deep. On other days, I was trippingly zipping through life, lighter than Holly Golightly. Ups, downs, highs, lows. Still, I kept going on the meds, off the meds, on, off, up, down. High today, then pushing that fucking boulder up the hill again tomorrow. Fucking Greek myths, man.

"Why do this to yourself," Doctor Blume asked one day, once again pursing her lips, leaning back in her chair, and cleaning her spectacles with the end of her sweater, just as she had on so many days before, as I reclined in her office, bedraggled, limp. After two years, desperate to shove off this crushing boulder from under which I couldn't breathe, I agreed with Doctor Blume's urging to stay on medication. My life changed.

There are four kinds of bipolar. I suppose most people think only of "bipolar 1" when they hear "bipolar," just as I used to. Although one may be the loneliest number, to paraphrase the Three Dog Night song, two can be just as bad, although when it comes to bi-polar, type 1 is the type of bipolar with extreme manic states, sometimes requiring hospitalization.

Names! Categories! Stupid, don't you think? I mean, if one with Type 1 has only mania–no depression–then how can that one with Type 1 be bipolar? Wouldn't she be unipolar? Or antipolar? Or just plain nonpolar? But we humans, we love our categories, don't we?

Well, at any rate, type 2–my type–has depression (mine mostly under control with medication), but the mania is milder, more of a "high" feeling rather than the kind of rollicking, out-of-control highs you might have seen Clare Dane's character, Kerry, in the hit TV show *Homeland* struggle with. I mean, I'm not going to stop taking my fucking medication because I think it will help me avert terrorist plots, like Kerry did. And even if I did stop, I wouldn't be inundated with overwhelming rapid-fire surplus uncontrollable thoughts which would enable me to foil international terrorist crises. Television shows! Movies! Stupid, don't you think?

I mean, don't get me wrong, Kerry was dope, but

nope, that's just not me. I'm just a quiet, gentle, nature-loving, vegetarian, classical pianist from Belarus. If I went unmedicated, I'd just feel a little high. Not coked-to-the-gills high, mind you. Not even close. More like the feeling you get on a summer's day, as you amble through Boston Common, the sun streaming satisfyingly between wavy weeping willows, calmly caressing cheeks, shining on white-winged warblers. No, I'm no Kerry, who sees invisible terrorist plots. But I do like threes. That's just because I'm an artist. Artists are quirky. Nothing to do with polarity. At least, I don't think so. I'm quirky, not coked to the gills.

"That can't be right," Doctor Blume suggested. "I just don't see how you can have three poles."

"I'm serious, Doctor Blume," I replied, "something is happening to me."

I adored Doctor Blume. She was a tall, trim, talented (three t's!) opera singer whose stage fright derailed what could have been a brilliant operatic career. With all that talent, she still became a psychiatrist. It's because of her curiosity about the world, and everything, especially everyone, in it (triple e right there!). I've always loved that about her–her bottomless curiosity. There was something innocent, sweet. Yet, so handsome, so serenely sensual (there I go with threes again!). And oozing oodles of (damn girl!) curiosity. There she sat, gracing her brown leather armchair, which should have considered itself fortunate to hold her. She was a painting. Cornflower-blue cashmere cardigan; perfectly pressed pomegranate wool slacks; short sassy socks with pictures of Diana Ross on them; impeccable black flats; skin as dark as the beautiful black blossom of a black hollyhock. She was always elegant, eloquent, erudite. Yes, she had those three e's wrapped up in a strong, self-assured, sensual woman (the three essential s's). She was beguiling, breathtaking, beddable (the three essential b's!). Beddable. Don't you love that word? What a great fucking word!

Have you noticed I like things that come in threes? Did I mention that? It has nothing to do with being a bipolar woman, bipolar the way. I am not a bipolar. There is no such thing as "a bipolar." I am a person, a woman, a classical pianist. I am a person with many a's who happens to have bipolar. There's a difference. In my case, perhaps three.

"What has happened?" Doctor Blume inquired quietly.

"Tatiana spoke to me."

Doctor Blume helped me beyond measure when I separated from my partner, Tatiana, two years earlier, not long after I started therapy. Things were so bad, so toxic, I don't think I could have lived much longer without change, a way to breathe. But then, about a year after the separation, Tatiana died from heart disease. She'd been diagnosed almost a decade earlier with a congenital heart condition, but it had since been under control with medication. I had been suffocating in the relationship for years, briefly breathed during the separation, then sadly started suffocating again, from remorse, after her death. Doctor Blume saved me.

"So, what has happened?" Doctor Blume asked. She studied me intently with her large eyes, the irises as green and textured as baby iceberg lettuces, irises that brought me back to the green, green grass fields in the French countryside, where my mother and I had briefly been immigrants when I was very young, before we came to Boston. We had fled Belarus, where life was harsh in the early post-Soviet days. After a year in France, my mother brought us to America, so I could study at the New England Conservatory of Music. How I adored those green fields, the lovely French country people, and Doctor Blume's green baby lettuces.

"It's Tatiana. She spoke to me, last night, while I was in bed. She said I should apply for the International Mussorgsky Competition."

"Yes, we've discussed performances before," Doctor Blume noted. "You're a brilliant pianist, Irina. The best I've met. But you can't play for an audience."

I hadn't been on stage for many years. Every time I tried to perform, it ended with me running off stage during the concert, sometimes making the bathroom in time. Sometimes, horrifyingly, not.

"So how can you play for the panel of jurists," Doctor Blume asked, "with a large audience, at the world's most premiere classical music competition?"

"Tatiana said she will guide me."

"You've never hallucinated before," Doctor Blume noted.

"Yes," I agreed. "And I'm not hallucinating now. What if there's more? Perhaps there's a–third pole. Something in me which is connected to something– more."

I've always seen things others couldn't. The energy fields in living things, especially plants. The colors in music. I hear the notes, of course, but also see their colors. Silly, do you think? For a very long time, everyone believed the earth was flat.

"Tatiana spoke to you? She was a wonderful pianist, so sad what happened. Still, I don't see how. I mean, the Compet-".

"She told me what to do," I interrupted.

"She did? But you two were in a very bad way together. Why would she want to help? You left, had to leave, to stay–to stay alive."

"Yes, I had to leave to stay. But she said all is forgiven. She's reached a new understanding. And I'm to play Mussorgsky's *Pictures at an Exhibition*. She'll show me how to win. The grand prize is four hundred thousand doll-."

"Wonderful piece!" Doctor Blume interjected, smiling broadly, her flashing teeth as white as the eighty-eight keys on my favorite Steinway grand. "I like the part when the music portrays all the little chickens running around, da-da, da-da, dum-de-de-dum-dee-dee, da-da," Doctor Blume said rapidly, as all ten of her long slender brown fingers scurried about the top of her desk like a frenetic feathered flock (three f's!) of Rhode Island Reds.

"But how will that help you win if you can't get past the opening cords without–forgive me–tossing your cookies?"

"Tatiana will teach me how."

"Could Tatiana have been a dream last night?"

"No, I don't think so."

"Why not?" she asked, leaning back in her chair, and again cleaning her smudged spectacles. For a moment, I thought she'd stripped off her doctor's cloak, that for a moment she'd let the willing suspension of disbelief allow her to believe that Tatiana really had spoken to me. Which she had. At least I think she had. Hadn't she? I thought for a moment that Doctor Blume could see that there are things in this world–and beyond this world–that science cannot explain. But no, instead, she continued methodically re-smudging her spectacles as she again asked the perfunctory psych doctor question.

"Well, Irina, you think it wasn't a dream–what makes you say that?"

"Because, Doctor Blume, I was awake."

She raised a finger, slowly opened her lips, paused, then lowered the finger. "Let's discuss this more at your next session," she suggested.

The next week, when it was time for me to again drop a dime on my brain–or have therapy, as some people call it–the door to Doctor Blume's office was cracked open when I arrived. Standing outside of her door, I heard her say, "Martin, yes, of course I'll be there tonight to have dinner with you, just like every night. I'll be there at six o'clock, just like every other day of the week."

Doctor Blume's younger brother, Martin, had a terrible stroke two years earlier. I read about it in the *Boston Globe*, which did a feature article about Doctor Blume's life and career. Martin lived in a nursing home since the stroke. Doctor Blume had originally planned to have Martin move home with her once Martin was released from the rehabilitation center, but then another terrible thing happened. Doctor Blume and her wife, Isabel, were driving home from visiting Martin at the rehab center. Isabel was a renowned violinist. She was texting a student when she drove their Volkswagen Jetta right into a telephone pole in downtown Boston, not far from their house on Sumner Street. It was December, just before Christmas. Ambulances and police cars screamed in the frozen night as they barreled to the accident site. Isabel was dead when they arrived; Doctor Blume had a broken collar bone. She recovered but fell into a depression. Unable to work for months, she lost the house and the rest of what money they had.

"I can't bring you home tonight, Martin. I'm sorry," I heard Doctor Blume say as I stood outside her office door. "Yes, I love you, too, Martin. It's just that I'm living in a studio apartment. Do you remember? Just one bedroom. Oh, you do? Good! Yes, Martin, I love you, too. Meatloaf tonight, how lovely! With gravy and peas? That's wonderful. I can't wait to get there. I'll see you at six. Yes, Martin, I love you, too. No, Martin, I won't eat any of your peas."

I heard Doctor Blume hang up the phone, then, a protracted sigh. I knocked on the door.

"Come in, come in, Irina. So, where were we last week?"

"You can help me," I said. "I just must know how to control my anxiety for the Mussorgsky. If I can manage my stage fright, I can play in the competition. And Tatiana said I will win. I have plans for the prize money."

Doctor Blume was silent for a few minutes. Then, "I want to help, Irina, but I have stage fright myself. It's why I gave up singing opera."

"That's OK, Doctor Blume," I offered. "I understand. You've been wonderful. Tatiana will guide me. I have plans for the prize money."

"Do you really need the money, Irina, since Tatiana had life insurance? You don't need to put yourself through this stress, do you?"

The rest of the session was mostly chit-chat.

Over the next few days, I gathered the materials needed for my application to the International Mussorgsky Competition. Application form, music resume, copy of passport, color headshots, a video of me performing *Pictures at an Exhibition*. I recorded this myself at M. Steinert & Sons on Damrell Street in Boston. Izzy, the store manager, let me use my favorite Steinway after hours. Just me, a wonderful grand piano, and my video recorder. It came off beautifully.

The next day, I uploaded the video and other application materials to the competition website.

Two months later, I received a letter in the mail. The postmark was from Moscow. My fingers trembled as I gently tore the end of the envelope. What if I was declined? Was my nighttime discussion with Tatiana just a dream after all? The letter read, in part, "... we regret to inform you that the Competition will not be held in Moscow this year. Due to the special operation in Ukraine, the Competition will be moved to New York City. The expert juries designated by the Organizing Committee of the International Mussorgsky Competition invite you to participate in the Competition ...." I felt my heart fill my chest.

I now had just three weeks to prepare to beat the pants off the other twenty-four pianist competitors. And the last time I'd been on a stage, at an afternoon performance of Rachmaninoff's *Rhapsody on a Theme of*

Paganini, even if I'd swallowed Sisyphus's boulder, it wouldn't have been heavy enough to keep my lunch down where it belonged. What began as Rachmaninoff ended as *Rhapsody on a Theme of Ravioli*. I cried for hours later that night. Doctor Blume was right – how could I win the Mussorgsky prize?

That night, as I patted the head of my ragdoll cat, Chopin, resting on my lap in bed, Tatiana spoke to me again.

"I know you will win," she whispered.

"But I can't handle my stage fright," I replied.

"Bollocks," Tatiana cried. "Here's the poop. As you're walking on stage over to the piano, take slow, deep breaths while you repeat a list of ten famous people who had bipolar."

"I don't know any famous people with bipolar."

"No problem, I'll tell you the list: Winston Churchill, Kurt Cobain, Patty Duke, Carrie Fisher, Vincent van Gogh, Ernest Hemingway, Vivien Leigh, Sylvia Plath, Frank Sinatra, Bruce Willis."

"Wait!" I cried. "Bruce Willis? The Bruce Willis? No fucking way! I love that man! But he's as steady as a rock."

"Are you kidding?" Tatiana asked, "did you see how down he was in *The Sixth Sense*? After being so up in *Die Hard*."

"Well, I'm not sure that's real," I said. I'm not even sure at this point you're real."

"Fine," Tatiana replied, "let's swap out Bruce Willis with Alvin Ailey. On another note, you'll need to go shopping."

"Shopping?"

"Yes, for a killer dress. To knock them dead at the competition. That's all you need. The music I'm not concerned with, you're a genius there. You'll see the colors in the pictures of *Pictures at an Exhibition*, just as you see the colors in musical notes. It's all connected, Irina."

"What is?" I asked.

"Everything."

"I'm not sure," I said.

"We just manage your stage fright and show off your outer beauty. The inner beauty, the musical beauty, is already there–it's you at the piano. And it's–perfect."

"Can I just choose three famous bipolar people?" I asked. "You know how I love threes."

"Yes, of course," Tatiana said.

"Tatiana," I whispered.

"Yes?"

"Why weren't you ... why, when you were alive ... how come you weren't, well ... kinder?"

"Well," she said, "I didn't understand."

"Understand what?"

"Everything."

The next morning, after scrambled eggs and toast at home with Chopin, I was off trying on dresses at the Gucci store at Copley Place. I fell in love with an azalea-colored sleeveless moire faille gown. Its watery pink finish fell in shimmering waves against my pale skin and contrasted perfectly with my long black hair. Looking in the full-length mirror at Gucci's, I saw I was quite smashing. The word beddable came to mind. I twirled in the dress in front of the mirror, pictured playing *Pictures at an Exhibition* in front of the esteemed jurists and audience. As I imagined them watching every inch of me, every fingering, judging every note and chord and pedal, every sustain and damper, every phrasing and articulation, I felt something deep within me stir. It was like a hard pit, a small boulder, rolling ever so slowly up, up, up my esophagus from where it was born deep within the acid-roiled Hades in my stomach. I began scanning the room to locate the bathroom before it was too late. In moments the lovely azalea gown would be a mottled egg mess.

But then I remember Tatiana's advice.

Carrie Fisher, Vivien Leigh, Sylvia Plath, Carrie

Fisher, Vivien Leigh, Sylvia Plath.

It was starting to work!

Carrie Fisher, Vivien Leigh, Sylvia Plath, Carrie Fisher, Vivien Leigh, Sylvia Plath.

If Carrie could save the galaxy, Vivien the south, and Sylvia confessional poetry, surely, I could save my breakfast.

Carrie Fisher, Vivien Leigh, Sylvia Plath.

I said it repeatedly, slowly, calmly, while in my mind's eye I watched myself play the opening Promenade of *Pictures*. I saw myself at the piano in the great hall of the competition. I saw myself playing beautifully and commandingly while I imagined roving through the art exhibition, together with Mussorgsky, who squeezed my hand excitedly as he talked about each painting. In front of the fifth painting–*The Ballet of the Unhatched Chickens*–Mussorgsky squeezed my hand even tighter as Doctor Blume whispered in my ear, "I like the part when the music portrays all the little chickens running around, *da-da, da-da, dum-de-de-dum-dee-dee, da-da*."

And as all of this was going on–as I saw myself playing in the competition hall while roving the art gallery in hand with Mussorgsky, while Doctor Blume hummed the dance of the chickens in my ear–I could see the colors of the notes Mussorgsky wrote. And I could see it was all connected. But I started to feel that pit again down deep in my stomach.

Carrie Fisher, Vivien Leigh, Sylvia Plath, Carrie Fisher, Vivien Leigh, Sylvia Plath.

"It's all connected," I whispered.

"What?" I heard Tatiana ask in my head.

"Everything."

I watched as I played the final dramatic movement, *The Great Gate of Kiev*. Followed by thunderous applause, a standing ovation. I saw clouds part, the cornflower blue sky, the sunflower yellow sun shining down. I twirled and smiled and hummed, and the colors of the dress and the cornflower blue sky and the sunflower yellow sun and the iceberg lettuce greens of Doctor Blume's eyes all swirled together with the blues and greens and crimsons and Russian reds of Mussorgsky's music. It really was all connected. *Everything.*

Either that, or I was coked to the gills. But no, it wasn't that, either. I'd gone off my medication. I needed to break free from the disorder of normality just long enough to see all the connections, to see the music colors, to win the Competition. I had plans for the prize money.

I charged the dress to my credit card, then hailed a taxi in front of Gucci's.

I arrived early again the next week for my session with Doctor Blume. Outside her office door, I once again heard her on the phone.

"Yes, Martin, of course I'll be there for dinner

106

tonight. Just like every night. I love you, too. Meatloaf again tonight? With creamed corn. How lovely. I can't wait. No, Martin, I won't eat your corn. Yes, I love you, too. No, Martin, I can't bring you home with me tonight. I'm sorry."

After I heard her hang up the phone and sigh, I knocked on the door. She welcomed me in and asked me to sit. She looked sad.

"How have you been, Irina?" she asked.

"I'm off my medication," I announced. "I have plans. I plan to win in New York. I need to see and feel everything. So, I stopped the pills for now."

"What about depression?"

"I'll go back on medication right after the competition."

"I see."

"Can you come to New York with me? Can you be at the competition?"

"I'd like to," Doctor Blume said, "but I have family commitments."

I don't think she knew that I knew about Martin. Psychiatrists aren't supposed to talk about their own private lives with their patients. Knowing that, I'd never brought up the Globe article I'd read, or the conversations I'd overheard with Martin.

"I understand," I said. "That's OK. Tatiana told me what to do."

The rest of the session was chit-chat.

I practiced for ten hours a day during the remaining two weeks before the competition. I took the Acela train from Boston to New York City the day before, and then a taxi from my hotel to Carnegie Hall the morning of my recital.

Tatiana's advice worked, for a few minutes, as I waited to go on stage. But then, no matter how many times I repeated the Tatiana mantra, Carrie Fisher, Vivien Leigh, Sylvia Plath, the roiling in my stomach overtook me. I dashed from the competitors' waiting area, chock full of nervous pianists, into the hallway, terrified that my breakfast was going to make its way up my esophagus and onto my lovely azalea dress. But thank goodness, I made the bathroom sink just in time. But then, a new problem. Walking back to the waiting room, I pictured myself stumbling on stage, to the piano, and, where I raised five fumbling fingers (three fs!) to play the few first dramatic notes of the opening movement, the Promenade, which establishes the musical motif to weave its way throughout the piece, linking all ten movements together, I saw myself stopping. Just stopping. Fingers poised in mid-air. In the waiting room, I repeated the mantra many times, took long, slow, deep breaths, and closed my eyes as I pictured myself strolling through the art gallery with Mussorgsky. I felt better, but still unsure I could go on.

Then a woman opened the door to the waiting room, leaned her little white neck and head in, and called my name. It was time. As I walked along the hallway toward the stage door, I felt the uneasy roiling in my stomach again. This was going to end, badly. I walked on stage, my gown shimming under the stage lights, the piano in front of me, seemingly as far away as a lighthouse in a distant harbor. I was on a little open boat, tossing in the churning Atlantic waves during a storm, the lighthouse right ahead but somehow a thousand nautical miles away. My musical career, my plans for the prize money, all those ten-hour days practicing, all the days and months and years of dreams and desires, about to drown underneath this oak ocean beneath my fashionable heels. I swallowed, hard, again and again, trying to swallow that Sisyphean rock, my fears, my doubts. Were the conversations with Tatiana real? Had she ever loved me? Had anyone? I swallowed again, harder. As I neared the piano seat, I repeated the calming words in my head.

Carrie Fisher, Vivien Leigh, Sylvia Plath, Carrie Fisher, Vivien Leigh, Sylvia Plath.

The choppy Atlantic waves beneath my feet slowly settled. *Carrie Fisher*. The waves smoothed. *Vivien Leigh*. Waves flattened into glass. *Sylvia Plath*. I took my seat at the piano. There was only me, now, I realized. Only me, this piano, and the calm soft ocean. I felt in command as I played the ten movements. I knew this music, these colors, this man, Mussorgsky. He linked the ten movements in a way that depicts a viewer walking through the art gallery, culminating in the grand, vast themes of the final picture. He spoke to me as we walked together through the art gallery, gazing at each picture. *The Gnome. The Old Castle. The Children's Quarrel after Games. The Ballet of Unhatched Chickens. The Market.* All the way along the gallery, until finally *The Great Gate of Kiev.* As we strolled, hand-in-hand, colors and notes and energy all swirled and melded into one before me. I kissed and chided and loved and scolded and merged with the eighty-eight piano keys. I saw, everything. The notes and colors and my fingers and Mussorgsky and my days whirling along green French fields and Doctor Blume's green lettuce irises and Tatiana's hair as yellow as a field of mustard and the cornflower-blue sky filled with floating clouds as white as the white light I first saw on the day I was born and perhaps will see again on the day of my death. I pounded the keys as my heart broke open during the final finale notes as I saw my heart spilling and painting the ocean beneath me a deep Russian red. I saw all of this and more. Everything.

The hall erupted into deafening applause after I played the final note. I stood, then bowed. Then I left the stage to wait in the wings with the other competitors.

After a half hour–or forever, hard to tell–a tall, dark-haired man in a black suit walked to the front of the stage from where he had been standing in the wings. He turned to the audience and, using a wireless microphone in his hand, announced to the audience the winner of the third prize, then the second, then the first. When I heard my name being read after the words "first place," I felt that rock roiling in my stomach again. I was about to lose my lunch in front of hundreds of cheering fans. Then I heard Tatiana's voice in my head:

Carrie Fisher, Vivien Leigh, Sylvia Plath, Carrie Fisher, Vivien Leigh, Sylvia Plath.

And the rock rolled back down to Hades.

When called, I walked to the center of the stage and bowed. The tall, dark-haired man in a black suit approached me.

"I am Peter Ivanovich Mussorgsky, grandson of composer Modest Petrovitch Mussorgsky."

"I am pleased to meet you," I said.

"Da," he said, "your playing–she is amazing. Like you talk with Mussorgsky. As if Grandfather spoke to you."

"Why, he did, Peter," I said, "he did."

Mussorgsky's grandson laughed awkwardly at what he perhaps assumed was my little joke.

"Ah, he spoke to you!" he laughed again.

I smiled at him.

Not long after, I received a letter in the mail from the Competition organizing committee. My fingers trembled as I gently tore the end of the envelope. Was Tatiana just a dream? Had I even gone to New York City? Had it all happened? The letter read, in part, "… the expert juries

designated by the Organizing Committee of the
International Mussorgsky Competition once again
congratulate you for placing first in the Competition ...."
A check for four hundred thousand dollars was included
with the letter. And an invitation to join the panel of
jurists at the Competition in New York. Next year, I
would be a jurist!

At my next session with Doctor Blume, I brought a
record, a copy of Mozart's *The Marriage of Figaro*.

"What's this about?" Doctor Blume asked as I
handed her the vinyl record.

"It's a gift," I explained.

"I'm not allowed to accept gifts from patients, Irina.
It's very lovely of you. One of my favorites. I always
preferred German opera over Italian. But as you're my
patient, Irina, well, I can't accept it."

"I can't be your patient anymore," I said.

"Oh, Irina, what makes you say that?"

"I'm moving to New York City. I've been invited to
be a jurist at the International Mussorgsky Competition.
So, you see, I won't be your patient now."

"Oh, I see."

"I wish you could come with me," I blurted out.

Doctor Blume pursed her lips– those lips I'd longed so

long to kiss–leaned back in her brown leather desk chair, removed her horn-rimmed spectacles, began polishing them with the end of her cornflower blue cashmere cardigan. Then, slowly, deliberately, softly, said, "Well, Irina, what makes you say that?"

"Because I'm in love with you!" I cried. "But don't worry, I know you can't come with me."

The rest of the session was chit-chat.

After leaving her office, I got a taxi to my apartment, where I began packing. Chopin and I were going to New York City! In my apartment kitchen, I filled a tumbler with tap water, and took my medication. I had lately been Holly Golightly again, happy go-luckily waltzing through my days, trippingly zipping through music competitions and doctor crushes and the swirl of colors and sounds and energies that make up–everything. But I knew the cliff was just ahead. And I wouldn't go over the edge this time, down, down, down into that blackest hole. I once again would don the cloak of normality. I would push out the colors from my sight and let in the everyday grayness. Of normal life. Of normal disorder.

Still, I smiled contentedly as I stuffed sweaters, socks, sheet music (four s's!) into my Samsonite suitcase. I smiled as I thought of my gift to Doctor Blume. Not the record (although it was a one-hundred eighty gram pressing with Irina Netrebko). Inside the record. That's where the secret gift was. And this note:

"Dear Doctor Blume, I don't know how to thank you.

113

There is no way to thank you enough. But, since I am no longer your patient, here is the four hundred-thousand-dollar prize money. I've endorsed the check to you. You can't accept it as my doctor. But you can accept it as my friend. Now, you and Martin can have meatloaf together, at home.

Your former patient and future friend,

Irina

P.S., Life's dope, don't you think? I do (that's three d's!)."

RICH GIRL

Tevye, the milkman, was on stage. The burly patriarch. The glue holding his family together, fighting to keep the modern world from encroaching on traditions, suffering at the hands of barbarous Russian Cossacks. As he began singing *If I Were a Rich Man*, Grace squeezed David's right arm. She leaned into him, whispered, "Dad, Dad, I can't believe they stole this song from Gwen Stefani!" David looked at her, gaze still riveted to the stage. She was so young, so innocent, so light, so—American.

"Yes," David said, flatly, "I guess they did."

He watched the show. At the end, the fiddler stood atop a roof on stage, playing a plaintive melody. David somehow knew, wherever life would now take him— home, prison, the grave—he would never see the fiddler again.

The day before, early morning of July Fourth, David was driving his black convertible, top down, to the nursing home where his grandfather Aleksey had been moved a few months past. Grace, just fourteen, graced the front passenger seat, the warm jet stream coursing through the open cabin, her long blond hair a field of tussled mustard. In the cramped back seat: a new king size pillow, encased in clear thick plastic; a wooden box of cigars; two carry-on suitcases for the flight from Boston to Manhattan later that day. The car whizzed along the highway while Grace belted out lyrics to the rap song

Rich Girl.

A morose melody—the theme from *Schindler's List*—
cut in on Grace's full-throated *Rich Girl* rendition. David's
cell phone ringtone. David pressed the button on the
steering wheel to answer the call hands-free.

"This is Tevye," he joked.

"Mr. Bernstein?" the woman asked.

"Yes, sorry, not Tevye the milkman. This is David
Bernstein."

"Are you bringing the new pillow?" the nurse said.
"Your grandfather dislikes ours."

"Of course," David replied. "It's right here in my
car."

"Fine," she said, flatly, then, "you should stop
bringing him cigars, Mr. Bernstein."

David glanced at the back seat, next to the white
puffy pillow, at the new box of Garcia Vega Blunts. The
only kind of cigar his grandfather smoked. The kind he
had smoked since time began. When David was young,
Aleksey chain smoked Blunts. He had no memories of his
grandfather without a stubby fat cigar in his mouth, or
delicately balanced between two fingers, as he flicked
black ashes into the clear, hefty glass ashtray on the table
next to the bespotted, century old armchair in his living
room.

Although David's grandmother died before he was born, the living room was still adorned with the wallpaper she had adored. Delicate pink roses on trellises. After decades of Garcia Vega soot, the pink had turned to battleship gray. But with Aleksey's move to Hemlock Ponds Rest Home, in Boston, a few months ago, the Blunts were now only allowed outside. This was an indignity for Aleksey which David felt sharply.

"He follows the rules," David told the nurse as he guided the convertible lickety-split along the highway. "He only smokes outside."

"Yes, but it's unhealthy," the nurse chided.

"He has an enlarged heart," David noted, "hardening of the arteries. Dementia. The clock is ticking. You want to take away his cigars?"

"I see," she offered coldly.

"How has he been this week?"

"It's getting worse," the nurse said. "He cries out at night."

"It's like he escaped from Ukraine yesterday," David mumbled, more to himself than to the nurse.

A day earlier, David had bought the largest, fluffiest pillow he could find, at Bed, Bath and Beyond. Then the box of Blunts at the beyond badly named local smoke shop, Smoke and Mirrors. Then he drove home and packed his bag for New York.

117

"It's time to go, honey," he called out to Grace, as he stood in his kitchen after breakfast next morning, pillow and Blunts box in hand. The carry-ons were already in the back seat. Grace was flitting about the house in the way teenagers often flit. Still too young for either her body or mind to be weighed down by regret, David thought. How he missed those days when he, too, was light. He smiled as he heard Grace, buzzing about somewhere upstairs, singing *Rich Girl*. It was a song she first sang years earlier. She'd loved it during its initial fifteen minutes or so of fame. Then, as with most songs, it was forgotten, at least by Grace. Now she was singing it again.

When Grace was nine, *Rich Girl*, a hit from Gwen Stefani's first album, topped the charts. Grace would bop about the house singing the lyrics with electric delight, her golden locks waving frantically, her fists pumping upwards as she punched holes in the sky. She had no idea, David had assumed then, that the song was a take-off of the original *If I Were a Rich Man* from *Fiddler on the Roof*. There was Gwen Stefani, on MTV and radio, singing a rap song about growing up in the hood in LA. Not exactly the original version from the musical about a peasant Jewish milkman in Ukraine, suffering from brutal Russian pogroms, fighting to preserve his family traditions as outside, modern forces encroached.

David himself was secular, quite removed from his heritage, and, as he delighted in Grace so much, he didn't mind the rap-hood shtick. What did offend him was bad grammar. It bugged David, the college business major, the persnickety accountant, that Gwen's lyrics were

118

grammatically incorrect. In Gwen's version, she fantasized about what her life would be like if she "was" a rich girl, instead of the grammatically correct "were" a rich girl. "You'll never get rich with that kind of grammar, girl," David had mumbled under his breath, knowing, ironically, that Gwen Stefani had indeed become rich at the expense of proper grammar. He didn't note the grammatical transgression to Grace, back then, because experiencing Grace's singing and dancing through the house warmed his curmudgeon blood. It warmed it five years ago. It warmed it again now.

David was taking Grace for her first trip to New York City, her first Broadway show. Afternoon flight on the Fourth, matinee on the Fifth. "You can pick any show you want, Grace," David had told her a month earlier. He knew there was a Broadway revival of *Fiddler on the Roof,* which had opened to rave reviews. So, he told Grace about when his parents first took him to see *Fiddler* when he was young. And about how it was–unexpectedly– played at his wedding, and at other major occasions of his life. His father played it on his record player when he was home dying of cancer, the year before Grace was born.

He even sometimes dreamt about the fiddler.

David didn't want to make the decision for Grace of which musical to see. He didn't want to be that father, the overbearing one.

"*Cats* is playing," he had told Grace, "and *Wicked*."

He wanted to see *Cats* or *Wicked* even less than he

wanted to listen to Gwen Stefani's grammatical bastardization of *If I Were a Rich Man*. But this trip was for Grace.

"I want to see *Fiddler on the Roof*," she replied.

He was surprised. Why her interest in such an old show, about peasant Jews in the old country, when there were plenty of modern shows to choose from? He'd raised Grace in a secular household. They'd never had a family Seder at Passover. Never been to a synagogue. Grace was further removed from Judaism than David was. He in turn was further removed from Judaism than was his father, who in turn was removed further than David's grandfather.

Aleksey was orthodox. He and David's grandmother had kept a kosher household. They held Seders every Passover. Attended synagogue every weekend for Shabbat. David's father also held annual Passover Seders, but he didn't belong to a synagogue, didn't attend weekly services, and, rather than orthodox, was secular, an atheist, a man of science. David had fond memories of Seder dinners and Chanukkah parties as a youth, but he had no connection to Judaism as an adult, especially since his father, Reuben, died fifteen years ago. David was just, American. And the first in his family to marry outside of the Jewish faith.

Grace's mother, Bridget, was Protestant, of Lithuanian, Polish and Irish descent. Bridget, too, was completely secular, an atheist, a woman of science—a psychologist. Each generation more American, until there was nothing of the old country left.

"I don't want you to choose *Fiddler* because of me," David had told Grace. He feared that his recounting for her the numerous times his parents had brought him to see *Fiddler on the Roof*, as well as the time his father snuck a bit of *Fiddler* into David's wedding, was unduly influencing Grace's indoctrinal Broadway show choice.

David had hired a classical violinist to play Bach and Mozart at his wedding. Only Bach and Mozart. As David and Bridget were exchanging vows, in front of a hundred guests, he heard, to his annoyed astonishment, *Sunrise, Sunset from Fiddler on the Roof*. Somehow, his father had got to the violinist. "Maybe my father isn't as removed from the past as I'd thought," David muttered when he'd heard the fiddler of *Fiddler on the Roof* intruding on his modern American wedding.

"This is your trip to the big city, Grace, you should pick what you really want" David had insisted. She wanted to see *Fiddler* had been her firm reply. A month later, suitcases and theater tickets packed and ready to go, they were driving to Hemlock Ponds to drop off a pillow and cigars for Aleksey before the airport.

Aleksey had been doing poorly in recent months. The dementia startlingly acute. Often not recognizing David. Often chattering as if he were still a boy back in Ukraine. David hoped that Grace would have a good visit, perhaps her last, with her great grandfather. That

Aleksey would be here, in the present, with her. He worried about bringing her, as she was sensitive, young, but he felt the chance for them to connect once more was too important.

David cringed as he pulled the convertible into the parking lot. He detested Hemlock Ponds. As far as he could tell, there were no hemlocks. And despite a thorough walkabout the property, no ponds. The building felt institutional. A humongous, rectangular, multi-story brick building with a thousand "apartments," which were, really, just rooms. Not the cozy cottages nestled on rolling hilltops ringed by thickets of hemlocks he'd pictured when he first heard the name, "Hemlock Ponds."

The most cringeworthy thing for David was the light system. Each resident had a small light on the outside of his or her apartment door, just above the keyhole. The lights, on timers, turned red overnight. In the morning, each resident was to push a button on the inside of the door, which would turn the light green. This was the residents' way of letting the staff know they were still alive. Staff began rounds starting at 10:00 a.m. If a light was still red, they'd knock on the door. No answer, they'd use a master key to enter and see who was dead or just sleeping in. David found this depressing. Red light, green light, dead or alive, welcome to Hemlock Ponds. Being the persnickety business major who didn't want Gwen Stefani to sing that she "was" a rich girl, he felt the nursing home had no right to call the place Hemlock Ponds, when the more accurate Waiting for Death Rest

Home was available.

Grace and David walked into the lobby. David had the new pillow under his left arm and the Blunts box under his right. They rode the main elevator up many floors, exited the elevator, began trudging down endless, narrow, windowless, dank hallways, each one identically papered with sepia-tone wallpaper. Following arrows, numbers.

Turn left, walk, walk, walk; turn right, walk, walk, walk.

Left, right, left, right, past hundreds of manilla-colored apartment doors, each nameless, identical, save for the diminutive black plastic apartment numbers on each. It felt more like prison than home, David always thought.

"There must be a retiree like me in every nursing home in America, I guess," David said, riffing on lines from his favorite flick. "I'm the guy who can get it for you; Garcia Vega Blunts, a bottle of Mogen David, a bag of weed, if that's your thing …"

"What are you talking about, Dad?" Grace asked. "Does Great Grandpa smoke weed?"

"No, honey. Blunts. Just Blunts."

1881

The little light by the keyhole of room 1881 was green. David sighed. He knocked, pressed his right ear on

123

the door when there was no response. He heard voices. A man's. A woman's.

Man: "Look, I don't know what's bothering you, but don't take your bedroom problems out on me."

Woman: "I have no bedroom problems. There's nothing in my bedroom that bothers me."

Man: "Oh, that's too bad."

David and Grace looked at each other. Grace shrugged her shoulders. David knocked on the door again. The man said, "The State Department could use her. What a party girl she'd make; in Moscow."

David turned the handle. The door was unlocked. He opened the door a wedge. He and Grace sidled in. Smells of urine. Lysol. Peaches.

"Great Grandpa?" Grace asked.

Aleksey was in his chair, an unlit Blunt dangling between two wrinkled, yellow, willow-fingers. He looks so small, David thought. Aleksey was watching the television sitting atop the desk on the other side of the little room. His chair was nothing like the lush, plush, once but not future king's majestic armchair in the living room of his house. No, this was a square, squat, steel frame affair, with a slim-jim thin black vinyl seat pad. Perhaps, David thought, the chair used to strap in convicted prisoners for their executions at Shawshank State Penitentiary.

David had desperately wanted to move Aleksey into an upscale retirement home at the time of the move, but the money wasn't there. David just didn't have it. He was barely squeaking by as a sole practitioner accountant, while also bleeding cash on attorneys for his divorce, which dragged on as interminably as a frigid Russian winter.

Though he'd seen it many times, David routinely surveyed the sum of Aleksey's "apartment":

One twin bed

Two white sheets

Two white pillows

One small television

One executioner's chair

One small steel nightstand

One Torah, black leather cover

One lamp, olive drab lampshade

Two open, empty boxes of Garcia Vega Blunts

One clear glass ashtray taken from Aleksey's home

Two framed photographs; one of Aleksey's wife, Edna, one of Grace.

Pillow Talk was playing on the television. The man

David and Grace heard from outside the room was Rock Hudson, the woman, Doris Day. A romantic comedy from 1959, the year of David's birth.

Aleksey looked away from the movie, glanced at David and Grace. His burnt caramel brown eyes raced wildly about the room, then settled unsettlingly on David.

"You're here to kill me," Aleksey said, matter-of-factly.

"Am I gonna see you tonight?" Rock Hudson asked.

"I'd love to, Rex," Doris Day replied, "but I already have a date."

"You're here to kill me!" Aleksey shouted this time.

"Grandpa, it's me," David said. "David, your grandson."

"You're here to kill!"

"No, I'm not," Doris Day said.

"And I ain't the kinda guy who'd ask you to," Rock pointed out.

David placed the pillow and Blunts at the foot of the bed, then walked the few feet to the television, turned the power knob off.

"I'm David," he said. "David."

Aleksey stared at David's face. He leaned his gaunt frame forward in the chair. The unlit Blunt, nestled in his wispy willow-fingers, flesh so paper thin it seemed to David that with a whoosh of air it would crinkle-crack open, slipped to the antiseptic white linoleum floor.

"David ... David ... it's you?"

"Yes, Grandpa. I'm David. I'm here with Grace, your great granddaughter."

David walked the few steps back to Grace and put his hands on her shoulders. Grace's pool-blue eyes welled.

Aleksey's eyes, still wild, in flight. "You must hide her, David. They're here!"

"There's no one else here, Granddad, only me. Only Grace."

"They're here now. We'll die. We must hide!"

Aleksey rose from his chair, feebly. With his walker, made his way to head of the bed.

"We'll hide now," he said, "we'll hide now."

David instantly knew he'd made a terrible mistake bringing Grace. He felt ashamed of his stupidity. He'd been hoping for her to have just one more visit. During his own visits in the few months since the move, David was startled by Aleksey's rapid decline. Sometimes lucid. Conversational. Sometimes, not knowing David. Every time, the desperate urge to hide.

David's father had told him the stories. How Russians had murdered men, women, children in Aleksey's village in Ukraine. Dozens murdered after rumors that Jews had used blood from Christian children in their rituals. When pogroms began in nearby villages, Aleksey's parents cut a large hole in their mattress. As the pogroms got closer to their own village, they'd hide Aleksey, just a few years old, in the mattress hole, then make the bed, until the Cossacks departed. Many times, David's father had told him, his grandfather hid in darkness, hour after hour, buried in the mattress. He was there one night when his parents were murdered.

An uncle fled the village and brought Aleksey to America.

It was thirty years ago, when David's father told him the stories. And the pogroms had happened decades before this telling. So long ago. Aleksey went on to have a good life here, David had thought. He met Edna. They married, had a little house, children.

The pogroms seemed to David like a chapter in a history book, the photographs black and white. A story, somehow, not real. And yet, now, here was his aged grandfather, curled in a fetal position, whimpering, looking for the hiding hole in his mattress. David could not bear it. How can this be? His strong, strapping grandfather, a burly blacksmith in his heyday. The family patriarch. The glue which bound together all the family.

Who fled murderous Cossacks. Who witnessed the worst, the ugliest, that people do. Who survived. Who overcame. Who, with a lifetime of healing, work, family, and love, thrived in a new world.

Now this disease, this vile dementia, in its own way as cruel as any Cossack. This disease, which took everything from him. Which took everything good. Which took away all the days, years, decades of love, family, healing, happiness. Which left his grandfather to hide, day and night, again and again. Which left him whimpering, fetal-folded, on the mattress, as he relived his parents' murders over and over in a vicious, cruel, endless loop. At the maddeningly named Hemlock Ponds Rest Home, which David thought itself was a vile mockery.

"No," David mumbled out loud. "No." David knew what he had to do. But how could he?

"No what, Dad?" Grace asked.

David did not speak.

"Dad?"

"Grace, why don't you wait in the car, sweetheart? I just want to talk with the nurse. I'll be right along."

He pulled the car keys from his jeans pocket, slipped them into Grace's hand, walked her to the door. In the hallway, just outside Aleksey's room, he whispered, "Don't worry, honey, everything will be OK."

129

"Are you sure, Dad?" Grace asked, clearly shaken.

"Yes, sweetheart. These things tend to come and go. I'll just talk to the nurse and be right along."

He watched her amble down the hallway, then begin to walk more assuredly, until she was swallowed again by the maze of carbon-copy corridors. Inside the apartment, David pushed the little call button on the wall of the bathroom. A few minutes later, a knock. He opened the door to let the nurse in. Aleksey was still curled on the bed.

"Is he like this all the time?" he asked.

"Most days. Sometimes he's quiet, other times he calls out. I'm sorry."

"Yes," David said, flatly.

He walked to the bed. "Grandpa, it's me, David," he said. "There's nothing to be afraid of."

Aleksey opened his eyes, looked sideways at David. "You're here to kill me," he said, matter-of-factly again.

"No."

"Who are you?"

"It's me. David. Your grandson."

"Whoever you are, you must hide!"

"Alright," David said softly, "let's hide." He covered

130

Aleksey completely with the white bed sheet, then walked quietly over to the nurse, standing by the door.

"It's alright," he whispered to her. "I'll stay with him."

He closed the door behind her, locked the deadbolt from the inside. He slid the executioner's chair over to the door and jammed it under the doorknob, since, he knew, the nurse had a master key. He stood by the door, his mind—somewhere else. It might have been a minute or few; it might have been a century. Then, at last, he said quietly, to himself, "no." He walked slowly to the foot of the bed. He glanced at Aleksey, still under the white sheet, completely invisible, hiding, cowering from Cossacks, as he did now every day, every night.

"No," David murmured. "No."

He wouldn't let an animal suffer so.

He picked up the new pillow, still encased in its plastic sleeve, from the foot of the bed. He stood next to Aleksey, clutching this, the best pillow he could buy, the pillow he'd hoped would bring comfort. He gently pulled back the white sheet, revealing his grandfather's head.

"Let's hide together," David said.

"I don't know you" Aleksey said, his burnt caramel eyes now looking vacantly at David's face, searching for recognition, finding none.

David stroked Aleksey's head gently. "It's alright,"

he whispered. "It's alright. You're safe now, no one is going to hurt you now."

"I don't know you," Aleksey murmured.

"I know," David whispered, "but hush, little boy, it's alright. I know your parents from the village. They sent me. So, you see, you're safe."

"We have to hide."

"Yes," David assured him. "Let's hide together."

David leaned down and placed the pillow over his grandfather's face. He pressed hard with both hands. The thick plastic felt surreal. Was he was home, in bed, dreaming?

"I know this is wrong," David murmured, crying. "To hell with you, God!" he blurted out, as he pushed and sobbed. "If there is a God." He pushed harder. "How *dare* you?" he asked. "How could you?" His tears made tiny serpentine tracks on the clear thick plastic encasing the pillow.

"How dare you?" he repeated, sobbing. He pressed the pillow with increasing firmness to match the degree of resistance from the other side. He held firm while soon the counter-push decreased. He held while the resistance was less, less, less – gone. Still, he held fast. Was it for five, for ten, for fifteen, for a thousand minutes?

David stood up. He unzipped the plastic case, removed the pillow. Placed it under Aleksey's head. He leaned down, kissed his grandfather on the forehead. He stood, blinking blankly at the wall ahead. Unsure of what happened. Unsure of who he was. Or what.

Then he remembered: Grace. She was in his car, waiting. He walked to the door, slid the chair from under the doorknob. He placed the chair where it belonged. Walked to the television. Turned the power switch on. *Pillow Talk* was still on air. David slipped into the hallway, closed the door behind him.

"Are you getting out of that bed," he heard Rock Hudson ask through the closed door, "or am I coming in after you."

"You wouldn't dare!" Doris Day exclaimed.

But he had.

Then David dove into the maze of hallways, following arrows to the lobby. "I must remain calm," he told himself. "Must go on. Must think of Grace. As if nothing has happened."

He smiled weakly at Grace as he plopped into the driver's seat. Started the engine. Turned on the radio. Drove to Logan Airport in Boston. He was on autopilot. He wasn't sure where he was. Not on this flight to NYC. Not in Ukraine in the village. Not in the old country. Not in the new. He felt as if he was floating though time, through space, like figures in a Chagall painting. He was neither here nor there.

He had to push on. For Grace. It was her turn now. Taxi in the city. Casablanca Hotel by Broadway. Matinee next day. Orchestra seats just five rows from stage. Grace's eyes blue saucers when the orchestra struck the opening chords. Her gaze riveted to the stage. David's mind was floating. Through time, though space, through Ukrainian pogroms, American playgrounds, weddings, divorces, first kisses, last kiss. The movie of his life was playing in vivid colors in his mind, but something was wrong. As Grace watched *Fiddler on the Roof,* he watched so many scenes of his life, but playing out of order, sometimes the scenes running forward, sometimes backwards. A divorce, followed by his first kiss, followed by the birth of Grace, followed by his father's death. It was all out of sequence. Out of time.

But the fiddler was there.

In the scenes he watched when his parents took him to dinner theater to see *Fiddler on the Roof*; in the scenes of his first wedding, when his father surreptitiously slipped an extra check to the violinist for her to play his favorite song from *Fiddler*; in scenes at his father's deathbed, when David placed a ruby red vinyl RCA Red Seal record of *Fiddler on the Roof* on his father's turntable. The fiddler was there, in all these scenes of his life, and many more. He had been there, in the background. Always.

THERE IS NO DEATH IN *FINDING NEMO*

Phil opened his eyes to see glass just inches from his face. He looked left, then right. He rotated his eyeballs three hundred-sixty degrees. He saw glass in all directions. Although the glass was clear, he could see smudges, and the lip running along the top of the bowl. He felt disoriented. He looked down: saw no body. Mary's digital alarm clock was next to him, on her bedside table. Is my head in a fishbowl? I must be dreaming. I'll just close my eyes and return to sleep.

Before drifting off, Phil remembered arguing with Mary over supper last night. It was a pitched, hurtful battle, starting, as it usually did, with the toilet paper.

"You left the toilet paper going the wrong way," Mary had said. "It's supposed to hang over the top of the roll."

"But I put the seat down," Phil said.

"Yes, but the toilet paper was wrong," Mary said.

"I don't want to talk about this right now," Phil said.

"You never want to," Mary said, impaling a Brussels sprout with her fork. "You never want to talk about anything."

"That's not true."

135

"Especially not about feelings," Mary said, "because you have no feelings. You're empty inside, Phil– just a head in a jar. Empty; selfish."

"Selfish?" Phil said. "Was it selfish when I offered to support your new pottery studio? How about when I said we could try to adopt, after the fertility treatments failed–after ten years and enough money for half a house?"

"You were always the master of the Grand Gesture," Mary said, "but you're selfish with your feelings. Do you even have them?"

"What the hell does that mean?" Phil said, raising his voice. "Jesus–it's never enough, is it? You've never been happy, Mary. You'll never *be* happy. I'm sorry we couldn't have children. I'm sorry the adoption fell through. I've tried to–"

"You have no emotional intelligence," Mary said. "I do all the worrying. I bear all the anxiety. You go to work, make money, that's fine, but it's all you do. That's not a marriage, it's not being on a team. Do you know, in our nineteen years together, I've never seen you cry? You're the only man in my entire life I've never seen cry."

"That's ridiculous," Phil said.

"Oh?"

"I cried when Nemo died," Phil said. "I cried quite a lot," he said, a bit smugly, whether because he thought he had just proved Mary wrong, or himself right, or perhaps because he thought he had just confirmed his humanity.

"Right, OK," Mary said, "once! Once, you cried, when the dog died. And what grown man calls a dog, Nemo?"

"Nemo is a fine name," Phil said. "And there's no death."

"What?" Mary said.

"There's no death. In *Finding Nemo*. It's a great movie, and a great dog name."

"Not for a *Great Dane*. You must grow up, Phil," Mary said heatedly. "Who has ever heard of a husband who won't cry in front of his own wife, except over a dog named Nemo? And, and, and–the *fucking* toilet paper. You always turn the roll around the wrong way, every time."

Recalling Mary's return to their eternal battle over the toilet paper roll caused Phil to roll his eyes, as his head floated in the jar, like Nemo darting in and out of plastic coral when he is imprisoned in a dentist's aquarium.

Phil closed his eyes. He re-opened them in Italy, sitting on a high window ledge, on a temperate Venetian morning. He opened the shutters, the better to see and hear the musician playing accordion as he strolled along the cobblestones below. The warm breeze fluttered the pink chiffon curtains across his cheek. He swept the curtains aside with the back of his hand as he looked behind him, at Mary, asleep on their honeymoon bed. As she rested atop golden satin sheets–hair the length of a hollyhock stock, as black as the impenetrable blackness of black hollyhock petals, as it trailed along the length of her long, bronzed limbs–he wished he could paint her portrait. He couldn't paint. Couldn't draw a straight line.

He looked out the window, at a man paddling a gondola along the side canal which ran by the hotel. Phil's heart ached with such bliss, he thought if he'd died on the spot, it would be just fine. He'd already reached the top of the mountain. If he fell off, so be it. There was nowhere higher to ascend. He knew this love would last forever.

"I'm in the mood for Chinese tonight," Mary said. She sat on the edge of the bed, flicked on the table lamp by the alarm clock and the fishbowl. "What do you think of cashew chicken with rice?"

"I don't think I've the stomach for it," Phil said.

"Coward!" Mary said, "it's not *that* spicy. I guess we could have Pad Thai."

"No, I mean, I haven't a stomach, at the moment," Phil said.

"You never did," Mary said, bitterly. She began to cry.

138

Phil closed his eyes again. He re-opened them at their wedding. Mary stood by him, beneath an altar of hollyhocks. They held hands, facing each other, in front of dozens of smiling, chattering family and friends, sitting on lawn chairs as they waited for the Justice of the Peace to speak. As Phil closed his eyes beneath the altar, he saw far into the future. There was Mary, resting in an armchair by the fire of their farmhouse. Her long hair was now silver, her face wrinkled, but sitting next to her by the fire, Phil saw only the raven-haired beauty shining atop golden Venetian sheets. Nothing had changed. Theirs was an undying love.

Children, grandchildren, and great grandchildren bustled noisily about on the farmer's porch, then came in twos and threes to give hugs and kisses and love—boundless love—to Mary and Phil. Then all were sitting at the long dining table. Platters of roast turkey, stuffing, and homemade cranberry sauce were passed from one smiling relative to another. Phil beamed. Surely his heart would burst. We've done well, haven't we? Look what a lifetime together has wrought. He leaned into Mary, and whispered, "we'll love each other this way forever."

"You're wrong," Mary said.

Phil opened his eyes to see the smudged glass, the clock, the lamp, and Mary sitting on the edge of the bed, eating Pad Thai with chopsticks from a white take-out carton.

"The crab," she said.

"What do you mean?" Phil said. "Pad Thai has crab?"

"In *Finding Nemo*, Phil. The crab. It dies. Eaten by a shark."

Phil closed his eyes. He didn't know what was real. He didn't know if he was dreaming. He hoped he was dead.

ABOUT THE AUTHOR

Jeffrey M. Feingold is a writer of short stories and essays in Boston. His stories have been nominated for the Pen America Short Story Prize for Emerging Writers, the Pushcart Prize, and The Best American Short Stories; finalist for the 2022 Eyelands Book Award; shortlisted or the Exeter Story Prize in England; and winner of London's Superlative literary journal annual short story prize.

Jeffrey's work appears in magazines, such as the international Intrepid Times, and in The Bark (a national magazine with readership over 250,000). Jeffrey's work has also been published in anthologies, and by numerous literary reviews and journals, including The Pinch, Maudlin House, Wilderness House Literary Review, Schuylkill Valley Journal, and elsewhere. Jeffrey's stories about family, about the tension between heritage versus assimilation, and about love, loss, regret, and forgiveness, reveal a sense of absurdity tempered by a love of people and their quirky ways.

Made in the USA
Middletown, DE
03 August 2023

35929136R00080